407-758-6701

HOT
STUFF

430.2320

HOT STUFF

JANET EVANOVICH
and
LEANNE BANKS

St. Martin's Paperbacks

This is a work of fiction. All of the characters, organizations, and events portrayed in this novel are either products of the author's imagination or are used fictitiously.

HOT STUFF

For information address St. Martin's Press, 175 Fifth Avenue, New York, NY 10010.

ISBN: 978-0-312-53160-7

Printed in the United States of America

St. Martin's Paperbacks edition / April 2007

St. Martin's Paperbacks are published by St. Martin's Press, 175 Fifth Avenue, New York, NY 10010.

10 9 8 7 6 5 4 3

Chapter
ONE

Cate Madigan had mentally stripped the guy across the table from her, and he'd come up short in every possible way. Cate hadn't actually *wanted* to see him naked. The image had just popped into her head. One of those awful moments of *too much information*! The guy's name was Patrick Pugg, and he was the Madigan family's pick of the week for a boyfriend for Cate.

Cate and Pugg were seated at the Madigan's chaotic dinner table, where the rule had always been *every man for himself*. Things had calmed down some since Cate's brothers Matt and Tom had moved out, but dinner here was still a harrowing experience . . . in a good Boston Irish kind of way.

There were eight people at the table tonight. Cate, Patrick Pugg, Cate's parents Margaret and Jim Madigan, Cate's older brother Danny, Danny's wife Amy, and their six-year-old twin girls, Zoe and Zelda.

The Madigans were all stereotypical Irish. Milk-white skin sprinkled with freckles, red hair that curled with length, brown eyes, a stubborn streak, and a natural bent toward practical jokes. The men were chunky and fought flat-footed. The women were slim and preferred getting even to getting mad.

Amy was the single frosted cupcake in the box of jelly doughnuts. She didn't look at all like a Madigan. Amy was the all-American cheerleader with blond hair, blue eyes, and smiley personality. Amy grew up half a block away and, from what Cate knew, Amy and

Danny had been together since they were two years old.

"You look all wrinkle-head," Zoe said to Cate. "What are you thinking about?"

"I was thinking about work," Cate said. "I need to go in early tonight."

This was a big fat lie, of course. Cate had been unconsciously grimacing at the thought of a naked Pugg. At five foot six inches he looked eye to eye at Cate. He wasn't bad looking, but he wasn't great looking either. Mostly he was . . . hairy. The hair crept from the cuffs of his shirt and spilled over his collar. He had long sideburns and a pompadour on the top of his head with a single curl pasted to his forehead. He was a car-crash cross between Elvis Presley and Squiggy from *Laverne and Shirley*. And he had a horrifying habit of referring to himself as Pugg.

"Pugg likes this pot roast," Pugg said to Cate's mother. "Pugg would like to find a woman to marry who could make a pot roast like this."

Cate's mother beamed at Cate. "Cate

makes a wonderful pot roast," she said. "Don't you, Cate?"

Cate blew out a sigh and forked up some mashed potatoes. She'd gouge out her eye with a rusted spoon before she'd make a pot roast for Pugg.

"Green beans," Cate's father said at the head of the table, and an arm reached across Cate for the bean bowl.

Food was circulating at warp speed around the table: the gravy boat, the dinner rolls, the butter dish, the green beans, the meat platter, the monster bowl of mashed potatoes. This was normal behavior at the Madigan dinner table, and over the years Cate had perfected the technique of passing with her left hand and simultaneously eating with her right.

"I heard the Sox are trading five guys," Danny said.

Cate's dad shoveled pot roast onto his plate. "Bull crap."

"I got something brown on my dress," Zelda said. "It smells like dookey."

"It's gravy," Amy said. "Don't worry about it."

"I don't like it. Make it go away."

"Dookey dress, dookey dress, dookey dress," Zoe said.

"Patrick sells tires," Cate's mother said to Cate. "He's the top salesman at his dealership."

Patrick Pugg winked at Cate. "Pugg is good at selling. Pugg is good at *lots* of things, if you know what Pugg means."

"No," Cate said. "What do you mean?"

Danny was seated next to Cate. You're baiting him," Danny said. "This is going to get ugly."

"Pugg's wounded," Pugg said. "Cate doubts Pugg's romantic virtuosity."

Danny stared openmouthed at Pugg for a beat. "Wounded? Romantic virtuosity? Who the heck *are* you? *What* are you?"

"I'm Pugg."

"Oh boy," Danny said. He slid an arm across the back of Cate's chair and leaned toward her. "Don't worry. I have a banker I want you to meet. I have it all set."

Patrick Pugg did a little finger wag at Danny. "Pugg wouldn't like that. Pugg is committed to making this relationship work."

Danny narrowed his eyes. "Did I miss

something? I thought you just met Cate to-night."

"Yes, but Cate likes Pugg, right? And Cate wants to see more of Pugg."

Everyone stopped eating and looked at Cate.

For the past six years Cate had been tending bar and working her way through college, inching closer to her goal of teaching grade school. Cate had always thought teaching second graders would be easy after living with three volatile brothers and tending bar. It was her observation that her older brothers, men in bars, and very young children had many things in common . . . for instance, they all from time to time exhibited inappropriate behavior, and they were all easily distracted.

If Cate told Pugg she wanted nothing more to do with him, he'd sulk through the rest of the dinner. If she told Pugg she liked him, Danny would sulk through dinner. So Cate did the only sensible thing . . . she accidentally on purpose tipped her water glass and jumped out of her seat when the water splashed everywhere.

"Shoot," Cate said. "Just look at this mess. I'm so sorry."

And she ran to get a kitchen towel.

"Good move with the water," Danny whispered when she returned. "It's a classic."

"It's all your fault. You caused that confrontation."

"Did not."

"Did so."

"Did *not*. Anyway, wait until you see the banker. He's light-years away from this moron. You're gonna like the banker."

"No. No more fix ups. I hate fix ups."

"I wouldn't have to get you fixed up if you were better at getting dates."

"I don't have time for dates right now."

"You're not getting any younger," Danny said.

"I'm twenty-six!"

"I worry about you," Danny said. "We all worry about you. We don't like you working in the bar, coming home at all hours, dealing with drunks all night long. You should be married to some nice boring guy who takes care of you and keeps you safe."

"I don't want to be married to a nice boring

guy. I want to teach school, and I want to marry an exciting guy who rides in on a big black horse and sweeps me off my feet."

"I'd feel better if he could ride in on a white horse," Danny said. "Why don't you at least get a better job? Something that doesn't dump you out at midnight."

"The bar is perfect. It pays well. It allows me to go to school during the day. And I'm good with the drinks and the customers. All those years of listening to everyone talk at once at the table are finally paying off."

Not to mention Cate was getting cheap rent because she was subletting a room from Marty Longfellow. Marty was a South End drag queen who sang at the bar and single-handedly pulled it out of economic disaster. Not only was Marty a fascinating oddity . . . she was also good. She had a voice like velvet and, after an hour and a half of shaving, two hours of makeup, a half hour to strap herself down and squirm into her dress, she was every woman's envy and every man's dream (at least on the surface). Marty sang at the bar two nights a week and traveled the other five, mostly doing private parties. Sometimes she would leave on an extended tour and be gone for a week or two. This was why Cate got the cheap rent. Cate guarded the castle. Cate watered Marty's plants, retrieved the mail, answered the phone, and made sure things were spiffy for Marty's return.

The perfect living arrangement, Cate thought. It allowed her to go through school without education loans. It got her out from under her parents' overprotective wings. And she had a big strong roommate who wasn't interested in women.

Cate mixed two mojitos. It was late summer and that meant exotic-drink season. Lots of margaritas and piña coladas and mojitos. A man at the end of the bar caught Cate's eye and lifted his empty glass. She handed the mojitos off to a waiter and sailed a Sam Adams draft down the polished mahogany bar. ESPN played on the television hanging over Cate's head. Conversation rose and fell in the dark room. Eyes occasionally flicked to the small, empty stage. Marty was expected to start another set in just a few minutes. Sunday night at Evian's Bar and Grill.

Packed with regulars, plus one new guy at the end of the bar, staring at Cate.

"Okay?" Cate mouthed to him.

He nodded and moved his hand in the hold sign over his draft.

Marty took the stage and there was a lot of hooting and clapping and yelling.

"Aren't you the shit?" Marty said to the crowd.

That led to more hooting and clapping.

Marty was six foot in heels. She was wearing a red sequined dress and a matching feather boa. She had a bunch of wigs, and tonight she'd chosen to have short black hair. Her red glossy lipstick matched her red glossy nails. Her eyelashes were long and fluttery and exaggerated for effect.

Gina Makin sidled up to Cate. Gina worked nights when Marty performed and extra help was needed. She had a husband and a one-year-old at home, and she was a primo bartender.

"She's wearing the Judy Garland wig tonight," Gina said. "I'll bet you five bucks she opens with 'Over the Rainbow.'"

Marty's keyboard wrangler, Slow Joe Flagler, banged out "The Wicked Witch is Dead" and Marty gave him the finger. Slow Joe grinned and went into "Over the Rainbow."

"The hot guy nursing the beer at the end of the bar is staring at you," Gina said to Cate. "Do you know him?"

"No. He's new."

"You should go flirt with him. He looks like fun."

"Think I'll pass on that. I've had about all the fun I can handle for one night," Cate said. "My mom invited another *Mr. Right* to dinner. He tried to kiss me when I left for work, I instinctively kneed him in the groin, and he said he liked a feisty woman."

"Obviously you didn't knee him hard enough."

"Seemed pretty hard to me. He went down to the floor and rolled around some before he said I was feisty."

Gina's attention was fixed on the hot guy. "Did he look like him?"

"Not even a little," Cate said.

The guy at the end of the bar was fine.

Black hair, styled short, but long enough from its last cut to wave a little over his ears and fall onto his forehead. Nice mouth, dark eyes, broad shoulders. He had his button-down shirtsleeves rolled to his forearms. Clearly he had some muscle. He caught her looking and his face creased into a full-on smile showing big-bad-wolf-perfect white teeth.

Cute, Kellen McBride thought, readjusting his former opinion of Cate Madigan. She looked like she should be tucked away in an old Celtic castle, wearing a flowing dress of emerald green, waiting for a knight in shining armor. He'd been watching her refill glasses and mingle with the regulars and had reached the conclusion that she was confident, spirited, and in control. This dragged a mental sigh out of Kellen. Cate Madigan was not the type who would ever need rescuing. She would make the dragon into a pet, defeat the villain, and use the moat of fire to bake cookies. Cate was, in a single word, enchanting. And the *second* word that came to mind might be intimidating. Not that any of this mattered. Kellen had a plan, and he was sticking to it until something better came along. He was going to finesse himself into Cate Madigan's life.

Kellen did a little *come here* crook with his finger, aimed at Cate.

"Me?" Cate mouthed.

"Lucky you," Gina said. "He's delicious."

Cate added to the tab for one of her regulars and ambled down to the hot guy.

"What can I do for you?" Cate asked. "Another draft? Bar menu?"

"It's what I can do for you," he said. "*Tai mina fhear chun tusa a thogail on gnathsaol.*"

This got a bark of laughter from Cate. "Okay, I'm impressed. This is the first time I've had a guy try to pick me up in Gaelic."

"Seemed appropriate. Do a lot of men try to pick you up?"

"No. I look like everyone's little sister. Mostly people try to get Marty's attention. And I know the translation to your Gaelic pickup line. You said I'm the man to take you away from everyday life. I appreciated the sentiment, but I actually like my everyday life . . . and sorry, I don't date customers."

Plus her mother's words echoed in her ears.

If a man is too easy on the eyes, he's likely to be hard on the heart. This had always presented Cate with a dilemma. Was she supposed to actually look for an *ugly* man?

"I have very good references," Mr. Hot Guy told her. "And my name is Kellen McBride. Your Irish father would love me."

"You aren't the banker, are you?"

"If I said *yes* what would it get me?"

Cate did an eye roll and moved to the other end of the bar to refill a wine glass.

Chapter
TWO

Cate was in the kitchen, making breakfast decisions, when Marty bustled in, fully dressed in black Armani slacks, Gucci loafers, and a white shirt that was left unbuttoned enough to display an elaborate gold chain. Marty was in man mode this morning.

"Omigod," Marty said, eyeballing the cereal box in Cate's hand. "Are you still eating that dreadful stuff? It's filled with chemicals.

It really has no redeeming value. And it'll go right to your ass and stay there."

"I love this stuff," Cate said, pouring out a bowl, admiring the pretty colors of the worthless, sugarcoated, puffed whatever. "What are you doing up so early? It's only nine o'clock. You always sleep until eleven."

"I have a long day. A meeting with my agent. Followed by brunch with Kitty Bergman." Marty grimaced. "Ick to Kitty Bergman. And a private party gig tonight."

The phone rang and Marty pressed his lips tight together. "Crap. I just know that's someone I don't want to talk to." His eyes fixed on Cate. "Sweetie, would you get it?"

Cate stuffed the cereal box into the crook of her arm and answered the phone. "Hello?"

"Is Marty there?"

The voice was deep and raspy. A man's voice. Either a big smoker or someone *very* old.

Cate gave Marty raised eyebrows. A silent question.

Marty shook his head no.

"Marty isn't available right now," Cate said. "Can I relay a message?"

"Tell Marty I'm not waiting forever."

"Great. You want to leave a name or number?"

"Marty knows who I am." And he disconnected.

"Some guy isn't waiting forever," Cate said to Marty. "You're such a heartbreaker."

Marty Longfellow lived in a building that had at one time been a dress factory. The exterior was red brick and sturdy. The interior had been gutted and remade into four floors of midrange, two-bedroom, two-bath condos. It was a South End address, and the inhabitants were a reflection of the eclectic mix of people found in that neighborhood . . . young professionals, gay men, and a smattering of senior citizens.

Marty's condo was on the fourth floor and was a candidate for *Architectural Digest*. The carpet was white plush. The furniture was black leather and chrome. The walls held original art. The chandelier was Murano art glass. Very beautiful. Very expensive.

Cate's single, small room to the rear of the unit was a candidate for *Yard Sale Digest*.

After paying tuition, buying books, and paying a token amount for rent, there wasn't a lot of money left for interior design. Cate had taken the yellow-and-white flowered quilt that had been on her bed when she'd moved out of her parents' house and coordinated it with Martha Stewart sheets, pillows, towels, and bath mat.

Cate's room was cheery, but not fabulous by Marty's standards. Marty had a sheared mink throw on his bed and thousand-thread-count sheets. And he deserved all of that luxury, Cate thought. After all, the man shaved off acres of hair every day. Plus, he moisturized, he conditioned, he worked out, he tweezed, and he lasered, peeled, and Botoxed.

It was midmorning and Cate was alone in the kitchen, frosting a cake. The phone rang and Cate gave it the fish eye. The phone was ringing on the hour, every hour. Three calls so far. All had hung up when Cate answered. She suspected it was the guy who was tired of waiting.

Cate snatched the phone and gave a curt "Hello."

"Yikes," Sharon Vizzalini said. "You sound cranky."

Cate had two best friends in the building. Sharon Vizzalini was one of them. Sharon was a realtor who lived one floor down in a condo crammed chock full of a former life. Four years ago, Sharon caught her husband bare-assed in the minivan with the babysitter. The very next day Sharon backed a U-Haul up to her four-bedroom, four-bath colonial in Newton. When the U-Haul couldn't hold any more Sharon drove it to Boston's South End, parked it in a lot, ran her finger down her listing sheet, and went condo hunting. Three weeks later she moved into Marty's building.

Sharon was older than Cate, and three inches shorter. She had curly black hair cut into a bob, a constant tan, a body toned in the local Pilates studio, and enough energy to make coffee nervous. Sharon favored animal prints for upholstery and clothes. She accessorized with big, clunky jewelry and didn't own sneakers. Sharon was total Dolce & Gabbana in slingback heels. Sharon wore heels to the Pilates studio.

"Not cranky. Just distracted," Cate said. "What's up?"

"I was hoping you could bring me a sandwich. I'm watching 2B. I think this is the day. I think he's finally going to walk out of his condo and show himself."

Cate swallowed a groan. Sharon was fixated on learning the identity of the mysterious resident in 2B. The unit had been bought by a holding company three months ago, and while occasional sounds and cooking smells oozed under the condo door, no one had seen the occupant.

"I love you, but you're sounding a little psycho," Cate said.

"It was bought by a holding company," Sharon said. "Only celebrities and mobsters do that sort of thing. Aren't you curious?"

"Curious, yes. Obsessed, no."

"That's because you don't have the realtor personality. We need to know these things. We worry about property value."

"I'm frosting a cake. I can bring you a sandwich as soon as I'm done."

"Cake?"

"Does that interest you?"

"Can I have some?"

"If you're willing to help me sing happy birthday to Mrs. Ramirez in 3C."

"The hell with 2B. I'll be right there."

Minutes later, Cate answered Sharon's knock.

"Wow, I could smell the cake from the hall," Sharon said. "Fresh-baked cake. From scratch. With frosting."

"From a mix," Cate said, returning to the kitchen and sticking a single candle into the middle of the cake. "But you got the rest right."

"I think it's great that you make everyone birthday cakes."

"It's my thing," Cate said. "I love making cakes. If I wasn't going to teach school, I'd be a baker. And I like Mrs. Ramirez. She's a good person, and I think she's lonely. Her kids have all grown up and moved away, and now it's just Mrs. Ramirez and her cat."

Sharon wandered into the living room while Cate tossed a handful of rainbow-colored sprinkles onto the cake top.

"Have you every wondered how Marty can afford this apartment?" Sharon asked Cate.

Cate pocketed her key and carried the cake out to Sharon. "Marty sings at the bar and at private parties."

"Yes, but look at this place. The furnishings are expensive and the artwork is signed. He has two Andy Warhol endangered species prints in this room. There's a Picasso series in the hall, and I remember when you took me on a tour . . . there's a Miro in the master bath! He has a Porsche parked in the underground garage. He wears designer clothes, and he has fabulous jewelry."

"Maybe Marty's family has money," Cate said, easing Sharon out the door.

"Does Marty ever talk about his family?"

"No. We've been roommates for almost a year, but we don't actually do much talking. Marty usually sleeps until eleven, and by then I'm either at class or at the library. I come back to the condo, make a peanut butter sandwich, and I'm off to work. I come home from work and crash into bed. And half the time Marty isn't even in town."

"Does he have boyfriends?"

"Probably, but he doesn't bring them here."

They rode one floor down in the elevator, exited, and marched to Mrs. Ramirez's door. They sang "Happy Birthday" to Mrs. Ramirez, ate some cake with her, and then they went their separate ways . . . Sharon to resume her surveillance of 2B and Cate returned to her condo.

Patrick Pugg was at Cate's condo door when she stepped out of the elevator.

"Pugg was afraid he missed you," he said when he saw Cate.

"I was just downstairs." Cate unlocked her door. "What are you doing here?"

"Pugg came to visit."

"I'm kind of busy right now."

"Pugg can come back later."

"Well, gee, I have to work later."

"Pugg can walk you to work."

"No."

"Pugg doesn't understand *no*."

"Shouldn't you be selling tires?"

"Pugg is on his lunch hour."

"You're probably a really nice guy," Cate said, "but I have to be honest. I'm just not interested."

"Pugg is crushed."

"The fact that I kneed you in the groin last time I saw you must have given you some indication."

"Pugg thought you were playing hard to get."

Cate slipped into the condo and closed and locked the door. She looked out the security peephole. Pugg was still there. Don't panic, she thought. He'll go away.

An hour later, Marty swept into the condo. "There's a hairy little man in the hall. He says he belongs to you."

"He's mistaken."

"Thank goodness. So far I've had a hideous day. My agent is a pig. He's going to have to be replaced. And Kitty Bergman is a bitch. I hate and loathe Kitty Bergman."

"I thought you loved Kitty Bergman."

"That was yesterday. Have there been any calls for me?"

"Someone's calling every hour and hanging up when I answer."

"That's not good," Marty said. "That's not good at all."

"Do you have a problem?"

"Heavens, no. Some razor burn on my chest, but aside from that . . ."

The phone rang, and Marty and Cate stared at it in silence.

"You should answer it," Marty finally said.

"Hello?" Cate said into the phone.

"I want to talk to Marty." It was the raspy-voiced guy again.

Marty was vigorously shaking his head . . . no, no, no.

"Marty isn't available."

"I know Marty's there. I saw him go into the building."

"Sorry, I haven't seen him."

"You're a lying bitch. Tell Marty I'm outside, waiting."

And he disconnected.

"He called me a bitch, and he said he's outside waiting," Cate said to Marty.

"This is a real pain in the ass," Marty said. "This is turning into *one of those days*. I'm going to go to my room and take a pill and pack."

"I thought you had a party tonight."

"I do. It's in Aruba."

Chapter
THREE

At ten minutes to five, Cate rushed out of the condo and ran into Pugg, still waiting in the hall.

"What the heck?" Cate said.

"Pugg got off work at four, so Pugg came back."

Marty was long gone, but an hour ago Cate had gotten another hang up, so she thought running into Pugg might be an okay thing.

Truth is, she was feeling a little freaked out by Marty and the phone calls, and she wouldn't mind having someone walk out of the building with her.

"Here's the deal," Cate said. "The boyfriend-girlfriend thing isn't going to work for us, but we could be friends."

"Pugg was in the market for a girlfriend."

Cate checked her watch. She was going to be late. "Pugg's going to have to settle," Cate said.

"If we're just friends, does Pugg get any?"

"Any what?"

"You know . . . whoopee do. Does Pugg get to hide the salami? Pugg has needs."

"Pugg's going to have to take care of his own needs," Cate said, heading for the elevator.

"Will you watch?"

"No!"

Seconds later, Cate was on the street, head down, power walking to Evian's.

"Cate has long legs," Pugg said, trotting beside Cate and breathing heavily, trying to keep up. "Pugg likes that in a woman."

Cate stopped outside the bar and looked at

Pugg. He was an obnoxious little bugger, but she had to give him points for persistence and a positive attitude.

"Thanks for walking me to the bar," Cate said.

"Pugg will stay here and walk you home."

"No walking home," Cate said. "None. Nada. No way."

"Pugg doesn't understand *no*."

Cate blew out a sigh and went into the building.

Thirty minutes before closing, Kellen McBride walked in and claimed a bar stool. Cate's heart involuntarily skipped a beat, and she mentally scolded herself about getting a grip. Okay, so he was a great-looking guy. And he was charming. And he was a flirt. All fun things, but no reason to get unhinged.

"Pick your poison," Cate said to him.

"Surprise me."

Cate drew a draft and started a tab.

"Not a lot going on tonight," Kellen said.

"Marty isn't singing. Customers always drop off when Marty isn't here."

"Are you friendly with Marty?"

"Moderately. Why, do you want an introduction?"

He shook his head. "No. I'm just making conversation. Don't want you to nod off on your shift."

Cate looked down the bar. Less than half the stools were in use. And no one required her attention. Everyone was nursing a drink and watching the overhead television.

"So what's a nice girl like you doing in a place like this?" Kellen asked.

"I'm putting myself through college," Cate said. "It's perfect. I work nights and go to school days. It's between semesters right now so I'm kind of lost during the day. I'm not used to having free time."

"I could help with the free time," Kellen said.

"Spoken like my brother's banker."

"I occasionally work for a bank, but I'm not a banker. And I don't know your brother."

"Swear on the blood of your ancestors?"

"That sounds a little grim, even for an Irish girl, but yeah, I swear. What's the deal with the banker?"

"My family is working hard to find me a husband. They mean well, but I don't want a husband right now."

Oh great, Kellen thought, doing a mental grimace. The woman had principles, worthy goals, and determination. Not only did she have those big, beautiful brown eyes, she had some intelligence behind them. Just what he didn't need.

"You have other priorities . . . like school."

"Exactly."

Cate caught movement in her peripheral vision and turned to catch Pugg motoring over to the bar.

"What's this?" Pugg asked, pulling up next to Kellen. "Pugg senses someone moving in on his squeeze."

Kellen looked down at Pugg and smiled. "Kellen McBride," he said, extending his hand.

"Patrick Pugg."

"I'm not your squeeze," Cate said to Pugg, her voice low, hoping to avoid a scene.

"Pugg has plans."

"Pugg is a nut," Cate said, just slightly louder.

"Many people have said this to Pugg, but Pugg is not deterred so easily. Pugg will be waiting outside to walk you home."

"No!" Cate said. "And if you tell me Pugg doesn't understand *no*, I'll have you bodily evicted from the bar."

"Then Pugg's lips are sealed, but you know what Pugg is thinking."

"I'm walking Cate home," Kellen said to Pugg.

"Pugg doesn't believe this."

"It's true," Cate said. "He's my . . . boyfriend."

"Pugg was told you were available. Pugg was told you were desperate for a roll in the hay. Maybe not in so many words, but Pugg felt it was implied."

"Kellen and I roll in the hay a lot," Cate said.

"Cate's mother didn't tell any of this to Pugg."

"She doesn't know," Cate said. "Kellen is a secret. I didn't think my mother would approve."

"Why wouldn't your mother approve?" Pugg asked.

"It's my job," Kellen said. "I kill people. It pays well, but it's not universally socially acceptable."

"Pugg thinks you might be pulling Pugg's leg, but then Pugg isn't entirely sure. You *could* look like a killer. Pugg will wait outside and watch from a respectful distance."

"Do I really look like a killer?" Kellen asked Cate.

Cate studied him. He had laugh lines at the corners of his eyes, but there was something else there, too. Grit, Cate thought. He was older than she was, and had seen more of life. And she suspected not all of what he'd seen had been good. "You don't look like a killer," Cate said, "but you look like you could kill if you had to."

There was no change in Kellen's expression. His eyes were steady and noncommittal, and his mouth remained soft with a hint of a smile at the corners. And Cate knew she was frighteningly close to the truth.

"I'll wait and walk you out," Kellen said. "Don't want you to look like a big fibber."

"Thanks," Cate said, wondering if she might not have been safer with Pugg.

• • •

Evian's closed at eleven on Mondays. Gerald Evian, owner in residence, dimmed the lights at 10:50, and the few remaining customers silently left their stools and wandered out. By five after eleven the registers were empty, the bottles were capped, and all the glasses were clean. Evian unlocked the door for Cate and Kellen, and they stepped out of the cool bar air into the warm night.

Pugg was waiting on the sidewalk. "Pugg decided there was something fishy going on, so Pugg is waiting to be convinced," Pugg said.

Kellen pulled Cate to him and kissed her. It was gentle and lingering, and there was just a touch of tongue. Not so much that Cate felt he deserved a knee in the groin, but enough to give her an unexpected rush.

"Okay," Pugg said. "Pugg is temporarily convinced. Cate didn't drop-kick Kellen when Kellen kissed her, but Pugg still thinks there's something rotten in Denmark. Are you sure you don't want Pugg to walk you home, too?" he asked Cate.

"I'll be fine," Cate said, "but thank you for offering."

"Pugg would put himself at personal risk for you. Pugg would carry you over mud puddles and walk on burning coals. Pugg would fly you to the moon."

"Gotta go now," Cate said, inching away.

"Pugg would climb the highest mountain. Pugg would rush into a burning building. Pugg would share his dessert."

Cate and Kellen were half a block away, but they could still hear Pugg.

"Pugg would kill spiders and snakes and slugs and yucky things. Pugg would let you spank him."

Kellen burst out laughing, and Cate clapped her hands over her ears and sprinted across the street.

Four blocks later, Cate stopped in front of Marty's condo building. "I'm sorry about Pugg."

"He's okay," Kellen said. "He's just trying too hard. He needs to chill a little." Kellen glanced at the building. "Is this where you live?"

"Yes. I sublet a room from someone."

"I don't suppose you'd want to invite me up."

"No, but I appreciate the rescue from Pugg."

"Another kiss?"

Cate smiled and key-fobbed the secure door open. "One was enough."

"Not for me," Kellen said. And it occurred to him that he might be in over his head on this one. He was liking Cate Madigan *way* too much.

The morning had been quiet so far. No threatening phone calls. No impromptu visits from Patrick Pugg. Marty was gone, and he hadn't been specific about his return. It was a little after nine, and in the silent condo, with little to distract her, Cate was having a hard time forgetting Kellen McBride and the kiss. Truth was, it had been a fantastic, spectacular kiss.

Cate's intercom buzzed, and her first reaction was to mutter a small prayer that it wasn't Pugg.

"Yes?" she said into the intercom.

"Delivery for Martin Longfellow."

Cate pushed the button to open the downstairs door. "Come on up."

Minutes later, when the doorbell chimed, Cate opened the door with her coffee in hand and gaped at the man and dog standing in the hall. The man was average height and weight, wearing a shirt that said Rudy's Security. The dog was a huge, slobbering beast.

"Dog delivery," the man said.

"You have the wrong apartment."

"It says here on the form that I gotta take him to 4A, and this here's 4A."

"Yes, but I didn't order a dog."

"Well, sweetheart, someone did." He ripped the top sheet off the form and handed it to Cate. "Looks like the dog was bought by a guy named Marty Longfellow. I got a packet for you too. All the papers are in the packet."

"No way."

"Your lucky day, huh?"

"He's going to have to go back."

"Sorry, no returns. It says right on the bottom of the form, Rudy isn't responsible for family disagreements. You bought him, and you got him."

"But I didn't buy him!"

"Does Marty Longfellow live here?"

"Yes."

"End of argument." He handed the leash to Cate. "Have a nice day, lady. I got a bag of food here in the hall. It comes with the dog. Rudy likes to see his dogs get off to a good start. Don't want him getting hungry and eating the dining room table, right?"

"You're kidding."

"Sort of." He threw the bag of food into the condo foyer and the dog took off for the bag. "Look at that," the man said. "He's making himself right at home." And he backed up and closed the door.

Cate wrenched the door open and caught a glimpse of Rudy's dog deliverer running down the hall. He punched the elevator button, the doors opened, and he jumped in. Cate blew out a sigh, closed and locked her door, and turned to the dog. The dog was sniffing around the bag of food, pawing it with his foot, and wagging his tail.

Cate opened the packet of information and shuffled through the papers. "It says here you're a Bullmastiff, and your name is Beast. That figures."

The dog's hair was short, and a mixture of brown and black. His nose was smushed in like a bulldog's. His ears were droopy. His neck was thick. His eyes were brown and soulful. He had a slight overbite and bags under his eyes. The top of his head was almost at Cate's hip, and Cate guessed he weighed maybe 120 pounds.

"This is bad," Cate said to Beast. "I know nothing about dogs. I've never had a dog. And don't take this the wrong way, but you're a dog and a half."

Also in the packet was a note-sized envelope addressed to Cate. She recognized Marty's scrawl, opened the envelope, and read the note.

Dear Cate,

I had to take off in such a rush, and then was so worried that you were alone in my condo fielding all those dreadful phone calls, that I took matters into my own hands and asked my friend Rudy to deliver one of his wonderful, specially trained guard dogs to keep you company. Not that I think anyone calling my number would actually be dangerous, but goodness, one can never be too careful these days. I know you'll get

*along famously with Rudy's dog and take good
care of him until I return. Give him hugs for me
and tell him daddy will be home soon.*

Marty

Cate turned to the wall and rapped her
forehead against it. *Bang, bang, bang.* "I
don't need this," Cate said. "School starts in
two weeks. What will I do if Marty isn't
home by then? What will I do *now*? I don't
think I like dogs. I've never had a dog relationship. And this dog is so big. And he's not
even attractive. And listen to me . . . I'm
talking to myself."

Cate dialed Marty's cell phone and got his
message service.

"Marty," Cate said, "I know you meant
well, but I don't *want* a dog. I don't know
what to do with a dog. And this dog is *huge*.
You have to get Rudy to take him back."

Cate looked at Beast. "Sorry you had to
hear that, but you've probably been there before. I bet you've been rejected a lot, what
with being so big and . . . you know, not
cute."

Beast stopped clawing at the dog food bag and looked at Cate. He shook his head, and slobber escaped from his floppy lips and flew in all directions. He tried to scratch his ear with his back foot and fell over.

Holy cow, Cate thought. This dog is beyond not cute. This is a dog disaster.

Cate called Sharon. "I have a problem. Marty bought a dog, and I've got him here, and I don't know what to do with him. Do you know anything about dogs?"

"I know that the food goes in and then the food goes out, and you have to scoop it up in a plastic sandwich bag or you get a ticket. And that's why I don't have a dog. What kind of dog is it?"

"Bullmastiff."

"Forget the sandwich bag. You want to go with the gallon size. I'm in the middle of something here. I'll stop over when I get home."

Chapter
FOUR

Cate called Julie Lamb. Julie was a transplant from Birmingham, renting an unfurnished unit next to Sharon. She slept in a sleeping bag on the floor. Her small secondhand television sat on a sturdy cardboard box, and Julie sat on a lawn chair. That was the extent of her furniture. She had two pots and a fry pan, and she bought her morning coffee at the coffee shop two doors down. She was

Cate's age and had worked as a waitress since graduating from high school. She'd had a dream one night that she should move to Boston, and the next day she followed the dream. That was a little over a year ago, and she was still wondering about the dream, waiting for something wonderful to happen. She worked nights as a hostess on the party trolley. During the day she sat on her lawn chair and put her thoughts to paper.

"Hey, neighbor," Julie said. "What's goin' on?"

"Marty bought a dog. It was just delivered, and Marty isn't home, and I have no idea what I'm supposed to do with him. Do you know anything about dogs?"

"We always had an ol' dawg at the house," Julie said. "I'll be right up."

A couple of minutes later Julie was in front of Beast, hands on hips, smiling. "Jest look at this here dawg! He's about the most adorable dawg I've ever seen. Look at his smushy face, and big brown eyes, and droopy ears."

Beast gave a happy woof, put his two massive front paws on Julie's chest, and they both went down to the ground.

"Woops," Julie said. "He's a biggun'."

Julie was a honey blonde with blue eyes and an Alabama accent so thick it was like a foreign language. Her hair was straight and long and almost always in a ponytail. She was average height and had an average girl-next-door body . . . if that girl lived in Alabama and ate a lot of fried okra and grits.

"He's supposed to be trained," Cate said, wrestling Beast off Julie. "It says on his papers he's a guard dog."

Julie got up and plastered herself against a wall so she wouldn't get knocked over if Beast got friendly again. "I don't know anything about trained dogs. Mostly we jest opened the door, and the dog run out. And then when he was hungry he'd show up on the back stoop."

"You didn't have to walk him and pick his poop up in a bag?"

"Not in my neighborhood. We was all happy if we didn't find old Mr. Lawson poopin' on our lawns. We jest let the dogs do what comes natural."

"I don't suppose you'd want to take Beast?"

"Sweetie, I'd love to take Beast, but my landlord made it real clear I can't have animals. I don't know why not. I mean it's not like the place is furnished. And what's he gonna do to an aluminum lawn chair? I'd be happy to go walkin' with you though."

"When do you suppose he needs to walk?"

"My guess is this dog *always* needs to walk. Look at the muscle he's got. He looks like my cousin Vern. Vern really bulked up in prison. By the time they let him out he had no neck. He looked like one of them big ol' gorillas. When's Marty coming home?"

"I don't know. He said he was doing a private party in Aruba, but he didn't say when he'd be back. Evian has him scheduled for Friday."

The doorbell chimed, followed by a fist pounding.

Cate looked out the peephole. "Oh no!"

"Who is it?"

"Kitty Bergman."

"That woman scares the bejeezus out of me," Julie said. "I swear she's the Antichrist. I know her and Marty are real good friends, but I never could see the connection."

"I know you're in there," Kitty Bergman yelled through the door. "I can hear you whispering. I can *smell* you."

Cate opened the door and Kitty stormed in. "Where is he? Where is that double-crossing misery of a man . . . or woman?"

"He's in Aruba."

"Aruba? What the devil is he doing in Aruba?"

"He had a private party there last night."

"I'm going to kill him," Kitty Bergman said. "I'm going to track him down and surgically remove his nuts, and then I'm going to kill him."

"Ouch," Julie whispered.

Kitty Bergman was five foot two inches tall, weighed exactly one hundred pounds naked, and had ass muscles that were so well toned they could crack walnuts. She was fifty-five years old and had been nipped, tucked, and sucked by some of the best cosmetic surgeons in Boston. Kitty was married to Ronald Bergman, heir apparent to the Bergman Corrugated Box fortune. The Bergmans owned a Back Bay mansion on Commonwealth Avenue, and while Ronald was off clear-cutting virgin forestland in a voracious hunt for yet more wood pulp, Kitty lived to fund raise. Kitty didn't give a flying fig about the various charities she supported, but she did love to see her sixty-thousand-dollar sparkling white porcelain veneers smiling out from the society page of the *Boston Globe*.

Kitty was hands on hips, platinum blonde hair lacquered into a tight knot at the nape of her neck, feet planted wide in Manolo heels. A Chanel purse hung on the shoulder of her aquamarine and crystal St. John knit suit. She leaned forward slightly and narrowed her eyes at Cate.

"I'm going to be on you like flies on a bad burger until you give up your precious roomie. I know you're in on this."

"This?" Cate asked. "What is *this*? What are you talking about?"

Kitty pointed her finger at Cate. "Don't mess with me!"

Beast pressed himself against the back of Cate's leg, doing his best to hide from Kitty Bergman. He looked out from behind Cate and whimpered.

Kitty gave Beast a cursory glance and made a sound of disgust. "Tsk." She turned on her heel, swung her StairMaster ass out of the condo, and slammed the door shut.

"Hoy cow," Julie said.

Cate tentatively patted Beast on the head. "It's okay," she said to Beast. "She's gone."

"Isn't this supposed to be a big, brave guard dog?" Julie asked.

"That's what it said on his papers. It said he was a trained assassin."

"Maybe he's just having an off day," Julie said. She fondled Beast's ear, and he smiled at her. "Then again, you might have gotten stiffed on the killer dog thing. He looks to me like a great big sweetie pie. I bet you got a guard dog dropout. I bet this here dog flunked people eatin'."

"Fine by me," Cate said. "I don't want a dog who eats people. It would be enough if he just *looked* scary."

"I guess he could look scary," Julie said. "But you're gonna have to get him to stop smilin'. I swear I've never seen a dog smile like that."

Beast wagged his tail and swept a crystal

bud vase off an end table. He jumped when the vase hit the floor and tipped the table over with his butt.

"Poor thing's just a bull in a china shop," Julie said.

Cate bit into her lower lip and stifled a hysterical giggle. If Beast belonged to someone else she'd be laughing out loud at his goofy clumsiness. Unfortunately he was sort of *her* dog, and she was mildly terrified.

"You don't want your dog steppin' on these glass pieces with his big ol' feet," Julie said. "Why don't you take him out for a walk, and I'll clean this, and then lock up for you. I'd walk him with you, but I was writin' in my journal, and I want to get back to it."

Cate pocketed her key and a couple of gallon-size plastic bags, and coaxed Beast out the door and down the hall to the elevator. They rode to ground level, and Cate dragged Beast through the lobby to the building's front door.

The instant Beast hit the sidewalk, his nose went up, his eyes went wide, and he bolted for the vest-pocket park across the street, dodging traffic, dragging Cate behind him.

He stopped short when his feet hit grass. He squatted and did a two-minute tinkle. When he was done with the tinkle he chased a squirrel up a tree, sat down in a patch of shade, and refused to budge.

Cate pulled on the leash, and Beast did a little growly sound. Terrific, Cate thought, *now* he decides to be assertive. Cate didn't want to annoy the trained assassin, so she sat on a bench beside Beast, and they watched the world go by. After a while Beast flopped down and fell asleep. An hour passed and Beast was still sleeping, but Cate was feeling restless.

"I have things to do," Cate said to Beast. "And this bench is getting uncomfortable."

Beast opened an eye, looked at Cate, and went back to sleep.

Kellen had been doing a periodic surveillance of the condo building and was caught off guard when he saw Cate sitting in the little park with the dog. His research hadn't included a dog, and he felt a stab of jealousy that Cate already had a virile male in her life. The fact that the male happened to have floppy ears, floppier lips, and feet that were two times too big for his body did nothing to help Kellen's cause. He was going to have to compete with a Bullmastiff. And, what was worse, he was going to have to shoehorn himself into Cate's bed because he suspected there wasn't a lot of room left after the dog climbed on board.

Kellen crossed the street and approached Cate's bench. He noticed the dog open an eye and give a nose twitch to check him out. The eye stayed vigilant, but the dog didn't move, and Kellen assumed he'd passed the first test.

Cate turned at the sound of footsteps, and sucked in some air when she saw Kellen McBride slide onto the bench beside her. The man looked damn good in the daylight. He was wearing a lightweight sweater with the sleeves pushed up to his elbows, jeans, and running shoes. His watch looked expensive. No wedding band.

"It's not a good sign when you sit on a park bench and talk to yourself," Kellen said.

"I was talking to the dog," Cate told him.

"Honey, the dog is asleep."

"I was hoping he'd wake up. I'm tired of sitting here."

"And?"

"I'm a little afraid of him. I don't exactly know how to get him back to the condo."

Kellen had his arm across the back of the bench, his hand lightly resting on Cate's shoulder. Friendly without being overtly aggressive. He smiled and leaned into Cate when he spoke, and Cate decided Kellen McBride was a master at inching up to the line separating acceptable behavior from *un*-acceptable behavior. Kellen McBride knew how to move forward without getting kneed in the groin.

"I have the feeling I'm missing important information," Kellen said.

"I rent a room from Marty Longfellow. He left for Aruba yesterday, and this morning some man came and delivered this dog. He's supposed to be a trained guard dog. Marty thought I needed protection while he was away. Problem is, I know *nothing* about dogs. And this one is so *big*. And clumsy."

"Why did Marty think you needed protection? This is a relatively safe neighborhood."

"Marty was getting some weird phone calls, and I guess he panicked."

"What's the dog's name?"

"Beast."

Kellen thought the dog looked more like a Floyd. He reached out to Beast, and Beast picked his head up and sniffed Kellen's hand.

"He's clumsy because he's young," Kellen said. "He's still a puppy." Kellen took Beast's leash and stood, and Beast stood with him. Kellen gave Beast a hand signal, and Beast sat and wagged his tail. "Good dog," Kellen said to Beast. Kellen looked at Cate. "I don't suppose you have any dog treats on you?"

"No. Should I?"

"It'll help if you reward him for good behavior. And if you're really in a bind you can bribe him. He's going to be a terrific pet, but he's too young to be worth anything as a guard dog."

"It said on his papers he was a trained assassin."

Kellen grinned down at Cate. "I bet you own swamp land in Florida."

Five minutes later they were all standing in Marty's condo.

"So this is where the famous Marty Longfellow lives," Kellen said. "Very nice. He's obviously making some serious money."

"He works hard," Cate said.

"You like him?"

"I do. We aren't close friends. We keep different hours, and Marty's away a lot. Still, he's a comfortable roommate." Cate unhooked Beast's leash, and Beast wandered off to investigate the condo. "Lucky you came along to help me," Cate said to Kellen.

"I live a couple blocks from here. I pass by that little park a lot."

"On the way to work?"

"Sometimes." Kellen went to the kitchen and prowled through cabinets until he found a large bowl. He filled the bowl with water and put it on the kitchen floor for Beast. Beast rushed in and drained the bowl.

"I have an appointment I need to keep right now, but I can come back at one and walk him with you. He should be okay until then."

"That would be great! Are you sure you don't mind?"

Kellen smiled at her. "Don't worry about

it. I like dogs. Although I might not be making the offer if you had a Yorkshire terrier named Poopsie, dressed in a pink sweater."

If I had a Yorkshire terrier I could manage this by myself, Cate thought.

Chapter
FIVE

"I stopped at the Barks-A-Lot pet store on Tremont and got some dog treats," Kellen said when Cate opened the door to him. "You want to hand them out sparingly. And I got you a book on basic commands. He's obviously been through obedience school. You should work with him a couple times a day to reinforce what he's learned."

"How do you know so much about dogs?"

"I always had a dog when I was a kid. And I worked with a dog in my last job."

"Which was?"

Kellen had a moment of hesitation. People always reacted differently when they found out. And he wasn't sure he was ready for all of the questions that would follow. Still, he was increasingly attracted to Cate, and he didn't want to screw things up by withholding any more information than was absolutely necessary.

"I was a cop," Kellen said.

"Wow. So that whole thing about you looking like you could be a killer . . ."

"This isn't a conversation I want to have at this moment," Kellen said. "And for the record, cops very infrequently kill people."

"Why did you change jobs?"

"It was too regimented. It turns out I don't always play well with others."

"And what is it that you do now?"

"Different things. Security sometimes." Kellen clipped the leash onto Beast's collar and handed the leash to Cate. "Let's walk."

"Were you a Boston cop?" Cate asked.

"No."

"Where?"

"My turn for a question," Kellen said. "How old were you when you lost your virginity?"

"Okay," Cate said. "I get the message. Let's walk."

Julie followed Cate into Cate's bedroom. "I saw him from my window," Julie said. "I saw you all go out with Beast, and I watched the three of you walk across to the park and walk down the block. And I saw you come back. And I rushed right up as soon as I saw Mr. Tall, Dark, and Yummy leave. Honey, he's delicious. Who is he? How long have you known him? Is he good in bed? He looks like he'd be *amazing* in bed."

"He's just a bar customer who took pity on me in the park when I couldn't get Beast to go home. I don't know much about him."

"I think you need to take him out for a test drive."

"I think I need to walk away and not look back. There's something about him that makes my radar hum. He's secretive. And he has a way of smiling with his mouth but thinking with his eyes. And he's much too good looking."

"Sweetie, there's no such thing as too good looking."

Beast rounded a corner and spied Julie. His ears went up and his eyes got bright.

"Uh-oh," Julie said. "Your dawg is gonna knock me down again."

Cate jumped in front of Beast and gave him a hand signal. "Sit!"

Beast sat and thumped his tail with happiness.

"Look at that," Julie said. "Bless his heart, he's all proud of hisself."

Cate gave Beast a dog treat. "Tall, Dark, and Yummy taught me how to do this. He worked with a dog when he was a cop."

"Tall, Dark, and Yummy was a cop? Oh, that's good news and bad news. The good news is there's nothing like a man in uniform, especially if he's carrying a gun. And the bad news is the statistics on cop fidelity aren't encouragin'. I know all about it because I used to date some of the guys who worked at the correctional facility in my town. And for a spell I dated Amos Cole, who was a sheriff's deputy. Amos sure could kiss. Trouble was he kissed *everybody*. I haven't seen him in a while, but my mom told me Amos had a premature bout of gingivitis and most of his teeth fell out of his head. Personally I think it might have had something to do with all that kissing. Amos kissed people in places I don't even want to think about. He was a kissin' fool. I heard Amos once Frenched Maynard Bailey's big ol' breeder sow, but that was never confirmed."

The doorbell chimed and Cate opened the door to Sharon.

"I came as soon as I could," Sharon said. "Whoa! Is this the dog?"

Beast looked up at Sharon and smiled.

"His name is Beast," Julie said. "And he's trained. He's probably smarter than half the people in my hometown. A lot of them we can't get trained at all."

Sharon tentatively reached out and touched Beast on the head. Beast gave a happy bark, put his two front feet on Sharon's chest, and straddled her when they both went down to the ground.

"See that," Julie said. "He did that to me too. He's probably trained to do that."

Beast was nose to nose on top of Sharon.

"Help," Sharon whispered.

Cate pulled Beast off and told him to sit.

"Sorry," Cate said, helping Sharon to her feet. "He's just a puppy."

"Yeah," Sharon said. "I could tell by the way he only weighs 120 pounds."

"Cate knows that because Mr. Tall, Dark, and Yummy told her," Julie said. "Mr. Yummy knows everything. And he used to be a cop, but maybe we shouldn't hold that against him until we know for sure how he stacks up on the fidelity issue."

"Tall, Dark, and Yummy?" Sharon asked.

"It's no big thing," Cate said. "He's a customer who saw me in the park and offered to help with Beast."

"I saw him out the window," Julie said, "and I bet you a dollar it's a *big thing*, if you know what I mean."

"Why don't I know about this guy?" Sharon asked. "Why does Julie know about him?"

"Julie knows about him because she's

nosy and hangs out her window all day," Cate said.

"That's true," Julie said. "I'm observin' humanity. I'm even observin' at night when I'm workin' on the trolley. I think people are real interestin'. And I'm good at observin' things. Like, I can tell somethin' went right for you today. You got a glow, and you didn't even cuss at Beast when he knocked you down."

"I sold a house today," Sharon said. "Sealed the deal a half hour ago."

"Woohoo!" Julie said. "That is so fabuloso. We should all go out and celebrate."

"I have to work," Cate said.

"Oh yeah, I forgot," Julie said. "Me too."

"We can celebrate after work," Cate said. "I'll make a cake, and we can meet here at 11:30."

"Perfect," Sharon said. "I'll bring a bottle of champagne."

"I haven't got anything to bring," Julie said.

"That's okay," Cate said. "You can bring yourself. We know you haven't got any money."

• • •

"I know you're going to be on your best behavior when I'm at work," Cate said to Beast, fondling his ear. "And I know your feelings are probably a little hurt because I'm locking you in Marty's bathroom. But here's the thing . . . this isn't my furniture. And even though Marty is the one who bought you, I feel responsible for keeping his condo nice when he's gone. There's lots of room in here for you. And I gave you a bowl of water. And there's a fluffy throw rug for you to nap on. And when I come home you can have some cake with Sharon and Julie and me."

Beast looked around his space. White commode and sink of space-age design, direct from Japan. Large walk-in shower. Large soaking tub with stainless bath caddy. Acres of Bulgarian yellow limestone. Fluffy white rug from a specialty store on Newbury Street. Single exotic phallic-looking red flower in a dark Asian pottery bud vase sitting on the caramel-and-cream onyx counter. Large bowl of water.

Cate closed the bathroom door and let

herself out of the condo. She rode the elevator to the ground level, walked out the front door, and stopped when she saw Patrick Pugg.

"Never fear. Pugg is here to walk you to work," Pugg said to Cate. "Pugg will protect you from ruffians and persons of questionable stability."

"At the risk of hurting your feelings, you're the only person of questionable stability I see on this street."

"That may be, but Pugg senses danger. Pugg is keenly intuitive."

"Does Pugg know any details about the danger?"

"Not yet, but Pugg thinks it will come to him."

Cate was walking fast to the bar, trying to get away from Pugg, and Pugg was scrambling to keep up with her.

"Let me know when you get the details," Cate said. "In the meantime, we should stop meeting like this."

"Is it your boyfriend? He's jealous of Pugg, isn't he? Pugg has encountered this problem before."

"It's not just my boyfriend. It's *us*. It's not going to happen."

"Pugg has encountered this problem before, too, and Pugg has discovered over the years that sometimes he can wear a woman down and eventually have his way with her. Pugg is not averse to pity sex. Sometimes women even have sex with Pugg as a bribe to leave them alone."

"That's disgusting."

"Yes, but effective. I don't suppose you would consider . . ."

"No!"

"Pugg suspects you'll feel differently next week."

"Pugg is cruising for another knee in the groin."

"Pugg likes your spunk, but he'd prefer not to get kneed in the groin again."

Cate wrenched the door to Evian's open and swished inside. "Go away," she shouted to Pugg. "Go home! Harass some other woman."

Cate went directly to the small back room reserved for employee lockers. She threw her purse into a locker and called her mother on her cell phone.

"Where did you find Pugg?" she asked her mother.

"I got new tires for the van, and he gave me a discount. He seemed like such a nice young man, I immediately thought of you."

"He's not nice! He's a disaster. You have to stop fixing me up. I'll find a man on my own. I'm just not ready yet."

"Your brother has a banker who sounds wonderful."

"I'm begging you. Please, no more fix ups for a while."

"I'll restrain myself. And Danny will probably lose interest in your love life since he has other things on his mind. Amy just found out she's pregnant again. I'm making chicken and biscuits stew as a special celebration dinner tomorrow night. It would be nice if you could join us and bring one of your amazing cakes."

"Sure. That's great. I'm really happy for Danny and Amy. And it's my day off so I don't have to jump up and leave before dessert."

• • •

Even before Kellen McBride strolled into the bar at ten thirty, he knew he was in big trouble. Cate Madigan was stuck in his head. He liked the way she smelled, and the way she kissed, and the way her hand felt in his. He liked her curly red hair and milky white skin and Opie Taylor freckles. She was all the things he admired and feared in a woman. And that translated to a knot in his stomach and an ache in the area of his heart. Symptoms very similar to indigestion, but Kellen didn't think an antacid was going to do much for him. He was very close to having his ticket punched. He supposed he'd always thought it would happen one day . . . he just hadn't planned on it happening now. Truth was, it was inconvenient and mildly painful. And he had no idea how to reverse the process . . . or if he wanted to.

"I thought I should show up to walk you home," Kellen said to Cate. "After all, I *am* your boyfriend. And I'm territorial. I wouldn't want Pugg moving in on me."

"Was he outside?" Cate asked.

"Yep. I told him I was on board."

"Did he go?"

"No, but he crossed the street."

Cate wandered the length of the bar, checking on the few remaining customers. A half hour to closing and everyone was in a holding pattern. She rinsed glasses and tidied up. And she thought about Kellen McBride, and admitted to herself that she liked him. A lot. And she was attracted to him. A lot. And she felt totally flummoxed over the whole thing. A lot.

"He's completely out of my league," Cate said.

Andy Shumaker dragged his attention off the overhead game to Cate. "Who?"

"Sorry," Cate said. "I was talking to myself. I didn't realize I was talking out loud."

"Why do you think he's out of your league?"

"He's way too handsome. And he's very smooth. He's probably had a kazillion girlfriends."

"Lucky duck," Andy said. "Who are we talking about?"

"The guy at the end of the bar."

"The one staring at you?"

"Yep."

Andy did a little finger wave at Kellen and hoisted his glass in salute. Kellen finger-waved and hoisted back.

Andy was in his midfifties and had recently been kicked out of his house. His wife had listed "constant humming and finger tapping" as grounds for divorce, and Andy was attempting to break himself of the habit by consuming large quantities of alcohol.

"I bet he exfoliates," Andy said. "I bet he's a stinkin' exfoliator."

Cate made a mental note to cut off Andy's beer supply for the night and slid a look at Kellen. "You could be right," she said to Andy. "He has wonderful skin."

"And look at his eyebrows. He has two of them. And they're not even fuzzy. I bet he plucks." Andy slugged down the remainder of his beer. "You know what it means when a man plucks his eyebrows?"

"He wants to look human?"

"It means he's gay."

"Feeling a little hostile to the well-groomed guy?" Cate asked Andy.

"I hate those groomer guys," Andy said. "They all think they're so hot. Look at the way his clothes fit. It's like he had them tailored. And his shirt is ironed. And he has muscles! I bet he works out."

"You could work out," Cate said to Andy.

"When?"

"You could work out instead of sitting here drinking beer."

Andy stared at Cate, mouth open, eyes showing mild horror as he digested her suggestion. The train was slow in loading at Andy's station.

Kellen crooked his finger at Cate in a *come here* gesture.

"Me?" Cate mouthed.

Kellen smiled and nodded.

Cate gave Andy a diet soda. "On the house," she said. And she moved down the bar to Kellen.

"You were talking about me," Kellen said.

"We were admiring your shirt."

"It's just a standard white button-down."

"It's ironed. Andy was impressed."

"As well he should be. What about you?"

"What about me?"

Kellen grinned. "Are you impressed?"

"Pretty much," Cate said. And she thought she would probably be even more impressed by what was under the shirt.

Chapter
SIX

Cate and Kellen stepped out of the cool bar into the hot night and immediately spotted Pugg waving at them from across the street.

"Pretend Pugg isn't here," Pugg called. "Pugg is a phantom in the night watching over his damsel."

"Pugg needs a reality check," Kellen said, taking Cate's hand.

Cate looked down at her hand in his. It felt nice, but she wasn't sure what it meant.

"Pretending to be a boyfriend?" she asked.

"No. I just wanted to hold your hand. I don't think we need to pretend anymore."

A light mist had started to fall and the sidewalk glistened under the globe lights that hung over Evian's front door. The temperature was in the low eighties. The sky was black and starless. The few people on the street walked with their heads down, plowing through moist, saturated air that clung to skin and soaked into lightweight fabric. It was a little after eleven and traffic was sporadic.

Pugg was still following across the street when Cate reached her building.

"Pugg's going home now," he yelled to Cate. "Call Pugg any time of the day or night if you need anything. Ice cream, pizza, chocolate bars, buttered popcorn, beef burrito, a morning diddle."

Cate felt Kellen's grip tighten on her hand. "I'm going to have to *talk* to him," Kellen said.

"Ignore him. He said he was going home."

Kellen released Cate's hand and moved to cross the street. "I'll ignore him after I *talk* to him."

"No!" Cate said. "You'll get blood all over your nice white shirt."

"I'll be careful."

"I hate this macho shit," Cate said. "Run Pugg!" she shouted to Patrick Pugg. "*Run.*"

"Oops," Pugg said. And he took off before Kellen could make his way through the street traffic.

Kellen turned back to Cate. "You ruined all my fun."

"You were going to hit him."

"Only if he didn't listen to what I was going to say."

And Kellen knew exactly what he was going to say to Pugg. Truth was Kellen liked Pugg, but Pugg was going to have to understand that it was unacceptable to speak to Cate like that. As far as Kellen was concerned, Cate was his, and he was prepared to protect her from all of the evils of the world. He was going to be the one to slay the dragon and storm the castle. Okay, so probably he would also have to sometimes pick up the dragon's droppings and take out the castle's garbage, but those weren't jobs for the faint of heart either, right?

"My brothers were always beating up my boyfriends. It was awful. After a while no one would date me. I had to go to my prom with my brother Danny."

"Pugg isn't your boyfriend."

Cate opened the front door to her building, and they both stepped inside.

"Next time I'll let you talk to him, but you have to promise not to hit him."

"Fine. Can I shoot him?"

Cate rolled her eyes and got into the elevator, and Kellen got in with her.

"You don't have to see me to my door," Cate said.

Kellen hit the button for the fourth floor. "Yes, I do. It's part of the boyfriend code."

"You're not actually my boyfriend," Cate said.

Kellen was standing very close. Close enough for Cate to feel his body heat. Close enough for her to catch a hint of something that smelled masculine and sexy and expensive. A lingering trace of cologne or aftershave.

Kellen closed the small space between them and brushed his lips across hers. "I *could* be a boyfriend," he said.

"Not afraid of my brothers?"

"I think I can hold my own."

"They fight dirty," Cate said.

"Me too," Kellen said. And he kissed her again, touching his tongue to hers.

Cate felt the heat rush through her stomach and head south. The elevator doors opened, and Cate debated staying in the kiss as opposed to jumping out and running for the safety of the condo.

"Can't make up your mind?" Kellen asked.

"I can handle Patrick Pugg. I'm not sure about you."

Kellen draped an arm around Cate and moved her out of the elevator, down the hall to her condo. "That's the fun of it. The mystery of it all, the thrill of the unknown, the challenge of the chase."

"I'm pretty sure I can handle the chase," Cate said. "I'm worried about the part where you catch me."

Kellen pulled Cate to him and kissed her, his thumb ever so slightly skimming the underside of her breast.

"Maybe we should get that part over with, so you don't have to worry about it," Kellen whispered into her ear.

"Tempting, but too late. I'm feeling a panic attack coming on just thinking about it."

Kellen grinned down at her. "I could get you liquored up first if you think that would help."

"A perfectly good suggestion, but I'm going to pass." Cate turned to her door and inserted her key. "I have a lot of Irish Catholic guilt and scruples to manage. I'm going to need some time." Plus a full personal disclosure and a physician's clean bill of health . . . in writing, Cate thought.

Cate paused with the key still in her hand. "This is weird. The door was unlocked. And I know I locked it."

"Maybe Marty came home."

"Marty is fanatical about locking the door. Especially if he's in the condo."

"Let me go in and take a look around. Wait in the hall."

Kellen stepped into the condo and flipped the light on. Cate followed him in and peeked over his shoulder.

"I thought I told you to wait in the hall," Kellen said.

"I didn't like that idea."

Kellen looked around. "Someone's been in here searching for something. How do you like *that* idea?"

"Are you sure? It looks okay to me."

"The couch has been moved. There are imprints in the rug where the couch wasn't put back exactly in place. Did you move the couch?"

"No."

"The drawer isn't completely closed on the buffet. One of the Warhol prints is a little crooked."

Kellen threw the bolt on the front door and walked through the rest of the condo. The master bath was saved for last. Kellen cracked the door and looked inside.

"Beast is still in there. He looks sleepy. I don't think he's a late-night dog," Kellen said.

"I'm really creeped out," Cate said. "Someone pawed through my underwear drawer and my cosmetics and Marty's underwear and cosmetics. *Ick!*"

"There are a lot of expensive things in this condo that would have been easy to steal," Kellen said. "Computers, handheld electronics, art prints, Marty's jewelry . . . although I suspect Marty's jewelry isn't real. And yet nothing was stolen that you can determine."

"I guess you investigated burglaries like this when you were a cop," Cate said.

"I didn't work burglary, but I know the drill. Since nothing seems to be missing, I'm guessing someone came in looking for something specific. Either they didn't find it, or else it was here, and you weren't aware of it."

"Good thing I had Beast locked up or they might have hurt him."

"Honey, he's supposed to be a guard dog. Remember, that's why Marty bought him."

Beast was whining and scratching at the bathroom door.

"I'd like to let him out," Cate said, "but I'm afraid he'll contaminate the crime scene."

"There's no crime scene to worry about," Kellen said. "No blood. No bodies on the floor. No hate graffiti. Nothing stolen. If you file a police report it will be convenient later if Marty discovers something gone, but it's not like the police will come in and dust for prints."

Kellen opened the bathroom door, and Beast bounded out and jumped around like a rabbit. Kellen took a dog treat from his pocket and gave it to Beast, who ate the biscuit and happily leaned against Kellen's leg.

"I have a feeling the intruder was looking for something Marty wouldn't admit to owning," Kellen said.

"What's that supposed to mean?"

Kellen shrugged. "Just a hunch. The phone calls, Marty's sudden departure for Aruba, the guard dog delivery, the break-in. It feels like there's something shady going on."

"I see your point. Problem is Marty never felt shady to me."

Kellen studied Cate's face. It was like porcelain, except for the small crease forming between her eyes. She was worried about Marty . . . more than she was about herself.

"Maybe there's something really bad going

down, and you need more protection than this dog. Maybe you need a former cop to spend the night," Kellen said.

"Nice try," Cate said. "I appreciate the offer, but it's time for you to leave. I'm having a party here tonight.

"And I'm not invited?"

"It's girls only."

There was a lot of loud knocking on the door, and Cate let Sharon and Julie into the condo. Beast immediately rushed over and knocked Julie down and sat on her.

"I swear this ole dawg jest loves me," Julie said. "I had a boyfriend once used to do the very same thing. His name was Euclid. Can you believe that? What the heck kind of name is Euclid? But I tell you he could smooch, and he had nice big paws on him like Beast."

Kellen scooped Julie up off the floor, and Julie's eyes got wide.

"It's you!" Julie said, staring at Kellen. "You're Mr. Yummy."

Kellen looked over at Cate and gave her raised eyebrows. "What?" he mouthed.

"Julie saw us walking Beast this afternoon," Cate said. "And she calls everyone Mr. Yummy."

"I was observin' humanity," Julie said. "I was watchin' the world turn."

Sharon was standing to the side holding a bottle of champagne in each hand. "Are you new to the neighborhood?" she asked Kellen. "Do you need a realtor?"

"Yes and no," Kellen said.

"Okay then," Cate said to Kellen. "I know you're on a tight schedule and need to get out of here."

"So, are you gonna be a boyfriend?" Julie asked Kellen.

"I'm trying," Kellen said.

Sharon gave him the once-over. "I hope you have good intentions."

"Yeah," Julie said. "Just exactly what do you intend?"

"I thought I might intend to take Cate out to dinner," Kellen said.

"I gotta give him, he's fast on his feet," Julie said.

"When?" Sharon asked.

"Tomorrow," Kellen said, smiling, looking at Cate. "Dinner tomorrow?"

"Can't," Cate said. "Previous engagement."

"What previous engagement?" Julie wanted to know.

"I'm having dinner with my parents," Cate said.

"Oh honey, it's your day off. You don't want to waste it havin' dinner with your momma."

"I promised," Cate said. "It's a special occasion."

"*Tuesday* is a special occasion for your family," Sharon said. "I've never seen a family do so much celebrating."

"You could take Mr. Yummy with you," Julie said.

Cate's heart stopped in her chest. "No way!"

"Sounds like fun," Kellen said to Cate. "What time should I pick you up?"

"No, no, no, no, no," Cate said. "It doesn't sound like fun. It would make the Spanish Inquisition look like child's play."

"Your momma would jest love it," Julie

said. "When's the last time you brought a boyfriend home? I bet it was ages. Mommas always love that kind a thing. Next thing they're buying bride magazines at the Piggly Wiggly and lookin' at weddin' dresses."

"Julie might have a decent idea here," Sharon said. "If your mother thinks you have a boyfriend she'll stop fixing you up with bridge trolls."

This caught Cate's attention. She bit into her lower lip and cut her eyes to Kellen. Her mother would love him. He was big and Irish. And he used to be a cop, so he was probably good at managing loud, crazy people like her family. Problem was she sort of liked him, but after a meal with the Madigans she was afraid he'd head for the hills, never to be seen again.

Julie and Sharon were standing hands on hips, waiting for Cate to make a decision, and Kellen was rocked back on his heels, hands in his pockets, smiling.

"An intelligent man wouldn't be smiling about this," Cate said to Kellen.

"I figure I haven't got anything to lose. If your family is nice to me I've got my foot in the door. If the dinner is a disaster I might qualify for combat compensation."

"You're starting to sound like Pugg," Cate said.

"At some level all men are the same," Julie said. "So whenever possible go with the one who's hot-lookin'."

"Okay, fine," Cate said. "Dinner is at six in Brookline."

"I'll pick you up at five thirty," Kellen said. "Do you want me to walk Beast before I leave tonight?"

Everyone looked to Beast. He was sprawled on the black leather couch, sound asleep.

"Thanks, but I think he's good for the night," Cate said.

Chapter
SEVEN

Cate absentmindedly swiped a spatula across the surface of the cake, spreading icing, automatically styling it into swirls. It was a spice cake with mocha icing. And this time the cake was scratch. It was midmorning, and Cate was working her way through her feelings for Kellen McBride. Did she like him? Yes. Did she trust him? Not entirely. Was he a hottie? For sure.

She hadn't told Sharon and Julie about the break-in. And she hadn't reported it to the police. Why? Because the more she thought about it, the more doubts she had that it actually took place. Okay, the door was unlocked. That could have been a lapse on her part. And the couch imprints didn't match up, but she hadn't vacuumed in days. Maybe the couch had been moved days ago, and she just hadn't noticed. It wasn't as if something had been stolen. It wasn't as if the condo had been ransacked by gorillas. Truth was, if it hadn't been for Kellen she wouldn't have noticed anything amiss, other than the unlocked door.

"So what do you think?" she asked Beast. "Do you think someone broke in here?"

Beast wagged his tail and panted. Beast wanted cake.

"Here's the thing," Cate said to Beast. "I've always felt safe here. I know Marty has an out-of-the-ordinary job, but he's really very stable. I can't imagine him mixed up in something unsavory." Cate scattered multicolored sprinkles on the top of the cake and added a yellow bow made from icing. "I just have this feeling there's a simple explanation for the odd phone calls Marty was receiving and the sudden guard dog purchase." Cate fondled the top of Beast's head. "I have to admit I wasn't overjoyed when you arrived, but I'm liking you a lot. You make the house feel homey. And you were a good boy today when we went for a walk. You only knocked down one old lady."

The doorbell rang and Beast followed Cate out of the kitchen. Cate looked through the security peephole and grimaced. Kitty Bergman.

"Well?" Kitty said when Cate opened the door.

"Well what?"

"Have you heard from him?"

"Marty? No."

"I see you still have the dog."

Beast turned tail and ran into the bedroom.

"He's shy," Cate said. "He's very sensitive."

Kitty Bergman had wormed her way into the living room and was looking around.

"Marty isn't here," Cate said.

"Just making sure." Kitty walked into the kitchen. "Who's getting the cake?"

"My family."

"Party tonight?"

"Dinner at my parents' house."

"Huh," Bergman said. Like maybe she didn't believe it. Or maybe it was barely of interest. Or maybe she had a lactose problem and phlegm in her throat.

Without invitation Bergman moved from the kitchen to Cate's bedroom. She looked in the door and Beast yelped and rushed out, knocking Bergman on her ass, leaping over her prone body.

"What the heck was that?" Bergman shrieked.

"That was Beast. I think you startled him."

Bergman was on hands and knees in her white Chanel suit and Manolo Blahnik slingbacks, scrambling to get to her feet. "That dog's an animal. He's a threat to decent people everywhere. You have some nerve harboring a dangerous animal like that."

"He's just a puppy," Cate said.

"He's a menace. Where is he now?"

"He's in Marty's bedroom."

"Are you sure he's not guarding Marty?"

"See for yourself," Cate said.

Bergman narrowed her eyes and swished off to Marty's room. She looked in and glared at Beast. Beast tried to fit under the bed, but he couldn't get all the way under.

"Huh," Bergman said, and she huffed off to the front door. "I'll be back," she told Cate. And she left.

"Lucky me," Cate said.

Cate got a dog treat from the kitchen and used it to lure Beast out of Marty's bedroom. She gave Beast the treat, sat him down in front of the television, and put cartoons on for him.

"Calm yourself," Cate said to Beast. "When I'm done with the cake, we'll go for a walk."

Julie was hanging out her open window, yelling at Cate.

"Y'all come to my apartment if you're done walkin'. I got a package for you."

Cate followed Beast into the building and into the elevator. They got off at three and Beast trotted down the hall to Julie's open door.

"Good thing I was in the lobby when the

delivery lady came through," Julie said. "On account of somebody needed to sign for this. It's from Marty, and it's from Puerto Rico! Can you imagine that? I bet it's something exotic."

"Marty is supposed to be in Aruba."

"Looks like he's movin' around. Hurry and open it," Julie said. "I'm dyin' to know what's in there. I never got a box from so far away as Puerto Rico. Once my Aunt Jane sent me chocolates from Los Angeles, but our cat Annie May was in heat and had a accident on the box, so we never did get to eat any of the chocolates."

"I never open Marty's boxes," Cate said. "I just leave them in his bedroom for when he comes home."

"Yes, but sugar, this box is addressed to *you*."

Cate looked at the box. It was marked FRAGILE, and it was addressed to Cate Madigan. "Marty's never sent me anything before," Cate said. "This feels odd."

"Jest have at it for heaven's sake!"

Cate ripped at the tape, opened the box, and found a lot of Styrofoam peanuts, an envelope addressed to her, and a large object shrouded in bubble wrap.

"What's the letter say?" Julie asked.

Cate read aloud. "This is for my baby Beast. It's a very special, one-of-a-kind water bowl for a very special doggy. Give him hugs and smoochies from me and fresh water every day. Tell him Daddy will be home soon. Love, Marty."

"Isn't that dear?" Julie said. "Who would a thought Marty'd be such a animal lover?"

"Knock me over with a feather," Cate said, tearing the bubble wrap, exposing a large, enameled sapphire blue dog bowl with "Beast" printed on it in bling lettering.

"It's beautiful," Julie said. And it's gonna look wonderful in Marty's kitchen. It's the perfect color. It's gonna match the little tiles in the floor. Isn't it just like Marty to want to coordinate a dog bowl?"

"I can't believe he's in Puerto Rico."

"It's so excitin'," Julie said.

Cate thought it was more disturbing than exciting. She wasn't happy to have Marty flitting all over the globe while she entertained an angry Kitty Bergman.

"Thanks for signing for me," Cate said. "I'm going to take it upstairs and wash it and fill it with water for Beast."

Ten minutes later Cate set the dog bowl on the tile floor. "I have to admit it's pretty," she said to Beast. "It looks terrific in Marty's kitchen."

Beast slurped up half a bowl and padded off to take a snooze. Cate looked at the cake on the counter and sighed. Danny was having another baby. That made three kids for her brother Matt in Atlanta. Two for her brother Tom in New Jersey. And now three for Danny and Amy. Cate was the holdout.

"But I'm the youngest," Cate said. "And I have goals and ambitions." She rolled her eyes. She was talking to herself again. And she was avoiding the real issue. The real issue was the guy on the black horse. The hero guy. "Okay," she said to herself. "I know I have unrealistic expectations. Even if the hero guy rode into my neighborhood, what are the chances he'd be interested in me? And even worse, what are the chances I'd be interested in him? For instance, suppose Kellen

McBride is the hero guy? It's a possibility, right? He's sexy and handsome and he's a great kisser. He seems smart. He was a cop, so he has to be sort of brave. And I'm even secretly kind of ga-ga goo-goo over him. He touches me and my stomach gets fluttery. So why am I dragging my feet?" Cate closed her eyes and thunked her forehead against the wall. *Thunk, thunk, thunk.* "Dumb, dumb, dumb," she said. "No guts. I'm a big chicken when it comes to the hero guy."

Cate was about to thunk her head some more when the phone rang.

"It's me," Sharon said. "I'm in front of 2B, and there's someone moving around in there. If I put my ear to the door I can hear him."

"How do you know it's a him?"

"I've got a feeling. Julie is here with me, and we knew you wouldn't want to miss seeing him come out."

"He might not come out for hours."

"Then I'll knock on the door and tell him . . ."

"Tell him what?"

"I don't know. I'll think of something."

"You have too much free time on your

hands. Maybe you need a hobby like growing orchids or woodworking."

"So sue me, I'm curious. Anyway, tell me you aren't nosy about this guy. Tell me you don't want to get a peek at him."

"Maybe a peek. Do you really think he's getting ready to leave?"

"Yes!"

"I'll be right down."

Sharon and Julie were sitting on the floor, backs to the wall adjacent to 2B when Cate stepped out of the elevator.

"I didn't miss him, did I?" Cate asked.

"No. He's still in there," Sharon said. "Get over here against the wall, so he can't see you through his peephole."

"Maybe he's a spook," Julie said. "Like a wanderin' soul. And that's why we can't see him when he leaves. He could just go under the door like a vapor. My cousin Charlene lived in a haunted house once. She said there was talkin' and everythin'. And sometimes things would disappear. My mamma always said it was Charlene's husband, Dale, who was takin' stuff and sellin' it so he could go to the dog races, but no one knew for sure."

Sharon leaned forward. "Shhh! I think he's at the door!"

In a fashion that would have made Lucy and Ethel proud, everyone scrambled to their feet and pressed themselves to the wall. The doorknob turned, and Cate held her breath.

"We're watchin' history take place," Julie whispered.

The door opened and an overweight man in overalls stepped out and closed the door behind himself.

Sharon had her hand to her throat. "Excuse me, sir," she said. "Are you the resident of 2B?"

The man looked at the unit he'd just left. "Me?" He adjusted his cap and shook his head. "No, I just fixed a plumbing problem. Had a bad float valve on a toilet."

"Is the resident in there right now?"

"Nope. It's a real nice apartment though. The guy's got a wicked sound system. Real good music collection too." He nodded and turned toward the elevator. "Have a good one."

Sharon started to go after him, and Cate

grabbed the back of her shirt. "Enough, stalker-girl," Cate said.

"But I had just a couple more questions."

"That's a big fib. You wanted to put him in a dark room, blindfold him, and make him recite everything he remembered about being inside 2B."

"Yeah, that's true," Sharon said. "I would have beat it out of him if he hadn't cooperated."

"This has been disappointin'," Julie said. "I expected to see some gangster or some reclusive individual. I'm goin' back upstairs and hang out the window some more. Maybe I can see 2B coming into the building."

"I don't suppose you saw anyone strange come into the building last night?" Cate asked Julie.

"No. I was working the trolley last night. I don't usually hang out the window after dark anyway. I saw a strange little man this morning though. He was standin' on the sidewalk, lookin' up at our building. He was a hairy little thing, and he had sideburns and a Kewpie doll curl in the middle of his forehead."

"Did you talk to him?" Cate asked.

"I asked him if he was a Kewpie doll, and he said *no*. He said he was a Pugg. I don't know what the devil he meant by that."

"It's his name," Cate said. "He's my mother's friend."

"He's kind of cute," Julie said. "Like a furry little forest animal. And he's short. It's been my experience that a short man with a little wee wee makes a real good lover. They gotta try harder than the big uns."

"He's sort of a nut," Cate said.

"Speaking of nuts, I saw Kitty Bergman drag her gloom-and-doom cloud into the building this morning too," Julie said. "She's here a lot, and she just comes on in. She doesn't have to intercom anyone to get past the buzzer door. How does that work?"

"She owns real estate here," Sharon said. "Two rental units on the first floor and one on the second floor."

Chapter
EIGHT

Cate stared openmouthed at the car in front of her.

"What?" Kellen asked. "Is something wrong?"

"This is your car?"

"Yeah, it's a beauty, isn't it? It's a '65 Mustang, totally cherried out in its original black paint scheme. It's got steel wheels and a K-code solid lift engine. And you don't have to worry about Beast in the backseat. The leather is practically indestructible."

It was a sign from God, Cate thought. Kellen McBride rode a black horse.

"It's a great car," she said.

Kellen smiled. "I got it as a bonus for a job I did last year."

Kellen opened the door, and Beast climbed onto the backseat and hunkered down. Cate slid onto the passenger seat and cracked her knuckles.

"Want to tell me about the job?" Cate asked.

"No."

"Just dandy," Cate thought. Black horse, sexy smile, hot body, dreamy eyes, and he was probably a hit man for the mob.

"Was it illegal?" she asked.

"No."

"Did it involve drugs?"

"No."

"Okay then."

Kellen stopped for a light and cut his eyes to her. "Are you worried about me?"

"Not anymore."

He reached over and held her hand. "Good."

"Maybe a little."

Kellen blew out a sigh. "I'm a salvage expert."

"What the heck is that?"

"I retrieve lost property."

"A repo man."

Kellen gave a bark of laughter. "I've never thought of it that way, but I guess it could apply." He brought her hand to his mouth and kissed it. "Are you still worried?"

Cate had the cake on her lap, and under the cake she pressed her legs together. "No. Yes."

"About my job?" Kellen asked.

"That too," Cate said. "You aren't one of those guys who go around breaking peoples' knees, are you?"

"No. I hardly ever break knees."

"That's a relief."

They were in a neighborhood of sturdy, modest homes on small lots. No garages. On-street parking. One block over was a street filled with small businesses, including the Madigans' store.

"My parents live in the cream-colored house with the green door," Cate said. "You'll never find a parking place on the street, but you can park in the back. There's an alley and room to pull in behind the house."

Kellen drove to the back of the house, parked the Mustang, and reached for Beast's leash.

"Are you nervous?" Cate asked Kellen.

"About meeting your parents? No."

"If you had any intelligence at all you'd be shaking in your boots," she said. "This isn't going to be pretty."

"Is that why you brought Beast? To take the pressure off me?"

"No. I brought him because my brother Danny is going to turn green with envy. He's always wanted a cool dog like this."

Cate's mother was at the back door, holding it open.

"This is Beast," Cate told her mother. "And this is Kellen."

"Good glory," her mother said. "I was expecting a little dog, and I thought you were fibbing about bringing a man."

"I'll put the cake in the kitchen," Cate

said to her mother. "You're on your own," she said to Kellen. "It's every man for himself from here on out."

Danny was in the kitchen. He gave Cate a hug and a bottle of beer, and eyeballed Kellen and the dog.

"I don't know about this guy you brought," Danny said. "But the dog is excellent."

Kellen stuck his hand out. "Kellen Mc-Bride."

"You're kidding," Danny said, shaking his hand. "You made that name up, right? Only leprechauns are named Kellen McBride."

"Behave yourself or there's no cake for you," Cate's mom said to Danny.

Zoe and Zelda ran in and flung themselves at Cate. She bent and hugged them, and introduced Kellen.

"Mommy and Daddy sleep in the same bed," Zoe said to Kellen. "Do you sleep with Aunt Cate?"

"Not yet," Kellen said.

"People don't sleep together until they're married," Danny said to the girls.

"Are you going to marry Aunt Cate?" Zoe asked Kellen.

"Maybe," Kellen said, his eyes smiling at Cate, showing nice crinkle lines at the corners.

Danny looked from Kellen to Cate. "Black horse or white horse?" Danny asked Cate.

"Black. Mustang. '65," Cate said.

Danny took a pull at his beer. "Huh," he said, not looking entirely happy.

Beast was beside Cate, eyes bright, tongue out, sizing up Zoe and Zelda.

"This is Beast," Cate said to the girls. "He's a Bullmastiff."

"He's big," Zelda said. "And he gots slobber on his mouth."

"That happens when he gets nervous," Cate said. "He's very sensitive."

"Why's he nervous?"

"Everything is new for him here. I think he's nervous about meeting you and Zoe."

Zelda put her nose to Beast's and looked him in the eye. "You don't gots to be nervous, doggy. I'm going to take care of you. You can watch television with me."

"He likes cartoons," Cate said. "And nature shows, but he's afraid of lions."

Zelda wrapped her hand around Beast's

collar and led him into the living room. "I bet you don't like when the lions go *roar* 'cause it's so loud," Zelda said to Beast. "And the lions gots too-big teeth."

"Do you come from a large family?" Cate asked Kellen.

"Four older sisters. Plus my grandmother lived with us."

"Were your sisters overprotective?"

"No, but for a bunch of years I used the next-door-neighbor's bathroom. We only had one in our house, and it was always occupied."

Kellen looked around and knew he was going to like the Madigans. Their house was a little worn down at the heels in places, but only because it was well used. It was overflowing with life, love, and family. The way a house should be. It felt a lot like his parents' house.

Margaret Madigan was working at the stove. She stirred a lump of butter into a pot of green beans and checked the two big deep-dish cast-iron fry pans in the oven.

"Biscuits are done," she announced.

Everyone grabbed food and marched into the dining room.

Cate took a seat and looked around. "Where's Amy?"

"She's upstairs," Danny said. "She gets sick when she smells food. She'll be down for dessert. It's the only thing she can eat."

"Can doggy sit in Mommy's chair?" Zelda wanted to know.

"He doesn't know how to sit in a chair," Cate said.

"He can sit on a couch," Zelda said. "He puts his hiney on it like a person's."

Jim Madigan buttered a biscuit. "What sort of work do you do?" he asked Kellen.

"Salvage," Kellen said.

"You mean like a junkyard?"

"No, sir. I work for banks and insurance companies and sometimes individuals. I investigate lost property."

"Like a private detective?"

"Sometimes the work might be similar. But I'm not a private detective."

A lightbulb suddenly blinked on in Cate's head. Kellen was using her to investigate

Marty. Marty had something someone else wanted, and Kellen had been hired to retrieve it.

"Omigod," Cate said, turning to look at Kellen.

"Uh-oh," Kellen said.

Cate narrowed her eyes. "I just figured it out."

"Can we discuss this later?" Kellen asked, voice lowered.

"Absolutely," Cate said. And she kicked him in the ankle.

Kellen dropped his fork and sucked in some air.

"Oops," Cate said. "Sorry. It was an accident." She kicked him again. "Oops, again."

Kellen wrapped his arm around Cate and whispered into her ear. "Kick me again, and I'll give Pugg your cell phone number."

"Might be worth it," Cate said.

"What's going on?" Danny wanted to know. "Is there a problem?"

"Nope," Cate said. "No problem. Just playing."

"So tell us about your folks," Jim Madigan said to Kellen.

"They're dead."

The table fell silent.

"I'm so sorry," Margaret Madigan finally said. "And your sisters?"

"They're dead, too." Kellen cut his eyes to Cate, daring her to kick him again.

"Any dead dogs and cats?" Danny asked.

"A few," Kellen said, almost smiling.

Cate was in the seat next to Kellen, arms crossed, eyes focused on a spot on the windshield. Beast was in the back, leaning forward, sensing impending doom.

"Not good body language," Kellen said to Cate. "You look angry."

"Madigan women don't get angry. We get even."

"Do I have more coming to me besides getting kicked in the ankle?"

"You have *nothing* coming to you. *Ever*."

"We're talking about sex, aren't we?"

"It would have been good, too. I was going to show you wild woman. I was going to do it all."

"All?"

"Almost all."

"Gee, that's too bad," Kellen said. "I was going to do a lot, too. Want me to tell you what I was going to do?"

"No!"

Kellen turned the Mustang onto Mass Avenue. "I might as well try to explain this while I have you captive. I'm an independent recovery agent. It occurred to me when I was a cop that the police do an okay job of catching bad guys, but do a very poor job when it comes to recovering stolen property. There are a lot of reasons for this, not the least of which are budget and focus. Too much crime, not enough cops. And frequently the stolen item is immediately fenced and passed along without a traceable record.

"Sometimes stolen property can be easily replaced. Sometimes it's irreplaceable. I go looking for the irreplaceable. Usually I'm employed by an insurance company that has taken a high-ticket hit. In this case, I've been retained by an individual who had a one-of-a-kind piece of jewelry stolen and wants it back."

"And you think Marty's involved?"

"If I run Marty's history over the last two years I find seventeen instances of theft occurring at parties Marty has attended. Marty is the only person common to all seventeen."

"Coincidence?"

"Seventeen is a lot of coincidence. Two weeks ago Marty performed at a charity function in my client's home, and the next day my client discovered an heirloom necklace had been removed from his safe. I've been hired to find the necklace. I was hoping I'd find it in Marty's condo."

"So you got friendly with me, so you could search the condo."

"That was my original plan. It was a lot more palatable than romancing Marty, but after watching you tend bar for an hour I wanted to be friendly just to be friendly."

"Sounds like a lot of Irish blarney," Cate said.

"Actually, I'm not Irish. My real name is Kellen Koster."

"Kellen Koster?"

Kellen had been slowly cruising Cate's

street, looking for a parking space. He found one half a block from the condo, angled the Mustang into it, and turned the engine off. "It was supposed to be *Kevin* Koster, but it got screwed up at the hospital and never got changed. Most people call me Koz."

"I'm not most people."

"I've noticed."

"Now what?" Cate asked.

"Now we get Beast out of the Mustang. He's panting hot dog breath on me. Then we mosey up to the condo and see where we go from here."

Cate took Beast's leash and coaxed him out of the car and onto the sidewalk. It was a little after nine and the city hadn't yet cooled down. It was cold beer and iced Frappuccino weather in Boston. Red Sox hats and funky T-shirts and sandals weather. And air so thick with hydrocarbons you felt a rasp in the back of your throat and felt the city grit against your eyeballs. All part of summer in Boston, and people were sucking it up at outdoor cafés and cheering at Fenway.

Beast plodded after Cate and patiently

waited while she keyed herself into the condo building.

"Well, good night," Cate said to Kellen when the door clicked unlocked. "It's been . . . interesting."

"You're not getting rid of me yet," Kellen said. "I'm coming upstairs."

"No way."

Kellen pushed the door open and stepped inside. "I want to search the condo again. And I wouldn't mind a good night kiss."

"Not going to happen."

"The kiss or the search?"

"Either."

Kellen got into the elevator with Cate and Beast and hit the button for the fourth floor. "Usually there's word on the street when an unusual piece is floating around. And there's no word on my item. I think Marty still has it. Somewhere."

"Why would he keep it? Doesn't that increase his risk of getting caught?"

"Only if he shows it. Most high-level thieves keep an item now and then for their personal collection. If they're smart they keep that personal collection hidden. And sometimes a piece is taken that's too hot to handle and has to be set aside for a year or two . . . or ten."

"Marty's condo has already been searched."

"I want to search it again." But mostly, Kellen thought, he just wanted a kiss.

Chapter
NINE

Cate plugged her key into the lock on her front door and the door swung open.

"Oh crap," Cate said. "Déjà vu."

Kellen stepped inside and looked around. "This isn't good."

Cate and Beast followed him into the foyer and gaped at the mess. Tables were overturned, furniture was askew, and couch cushions were on the floor.

"This wasn't a normal search," Kellen said, walking through the condo. "It looks to me like there was a fight here. There's a spray of blood droplets on the kitchen floor, like someone was punched in the nose."

"That makes no sense."

"Maybe Marty returned and someone followed him."

"I can't see Marty leaving the front door open or walking away from blood on the floor. Marty is fastidious."

"Maybe Marty didn't *walk* away."

A half hour later Cate and Kellen were in Marty's small office, and Kellen was in Marty's desk chair, rifling through Marty's drawers.

"Nothing of any value in his file cabinet," Kellen said. "His computer is traveling with him. I can't find any memory sticks or disks or safety deposit box keys. No James Bond fake drawers or revolving bookcases. This office is clean. In fact, so far as I can see the whole condo is clean. And I don't believe it. I know I'm missing something."

"You're nothing if not tenacious," Cate said.

Kellen smiled slyly. "Something to remember. I could make Pugg look like an amateur."

"Should we call the police?"

"Yeah. This is the second break-in and someone bled all over your floor. It wouldn't hurt to have a report on record."

"Will the police test the blood?"

"Not unless they find a body in the stairwell."

Cate and Kellen locked eyes.

"Maybe I should check the stairwell," Kellen said.

Cate pocketed the key to the condo front door and followed Kellen into the stairwell. It was well lit, and it was easy to see that the stairs were speckled with tiny dark dots.

"Blood?" Cate asked.

Kellen was stopped at the third-floor landing. "Lots of it. And a dead guy."

Cate caught up to him and clapped a hand over her mouth. There was a large man lying in an awkward position on the landing floor. He was Caucasian, with brown hair and a severely receding hairline. Late forties. Dressed in a short-sleeved white dress shirt and brown slacks. He was on his stomach with his legs twisted at odd angles. His head was turned to the ceiling. He looked surprised. Blood had pooled under him.

"You aren't going to scream or faint or throw up, are you?" Kellen asked.

"I'm not going to scream, but I might throw up."

"Sit down and take some deep breaths."

"Are you sure he's dead?" Cate asked.

"His head is on backward. That usually indicates death."

Cate crept closer. "Looks like he's the one who got punched in the nose. Guess that's the least of his problems now."

"I don't see any bullet holes or knife wounds. It almost looks like he fell down the stairs and broke his neck. Do you know him?"

"I think he might be Marty's agent. I don't remember his name. I've only seen him a couple times, when he came to the bar to hear Marty sing."

"Go back upstairs," Kellen said. "We definitely need to call the police."

• • •

Cate looked past the young detective talking to Kellen and spotted Julie and Sharon standing in the hall with a cluster of curious condo residents. Sharon was wearing her robe and jammies, and three-inch stiletto-heeled slippers. Julie was in her party trolley attire of white Party Trolley T-shirt and black jeans.

Cate waved to Julie and Sharon, and they broke from the group and joined Cate in the condo.

"We came as soon as we figured it out," Sharon said. "Julie saw the police when she came home from work."

"At first I thought it was a domestic disturbance," Julie said. "You know how the Millers are always yellin' at each other and threatenin' to call the police. But then I saw them cart someone out in a body bag, and I called Sharon."

"This is horrible," Sharon said. "Do you have any idea what something like this can do to property values?" She paused for a moment. "On the other hand, if the person in the body bag lived here, there could be a unit going up for sale. I might be able to get the listing if I move fast."

"I don't think he lived here," Cate said.

"Did you see him?" Julie asked. "I bet you know all the details about the deceased."

"Not a lot of details to know," Cate said. "Kellen and I discovered him in the stairwell. It looked like he'd fallen down the stairs."

"That's tragic," Julie said. "Bodies are so fragile. One minute they're walking around and then *bang*, they're all broken. And fate is capricious. I just learned that word today and I'm not sure I used it right."

Sharon leaned toward Julie. "Have you been drinking?"

"They were serving margaritas on the trolley, and they mixed up too many, so when everyone left I had to drink some."

"You *had* to?"

"It was the polite thing to do."

Sharon turned to Cate. "If you found the body in the stairwell, why are the police swarming all over your condo?"

"It's possible that the dead man was in here first. My door was unlocked and things were disrupted."

"That's sooo creepy," Julie said. "I'd totally freak if I thought a dead man had been walking around in my apartment. My Aunt Margery kept my Uncle Lester in the living room for two months after he died. She said it kept her from gettin' lonely. Of course he didn't walk around, but he was there all the same, laid out on the living room couch. Truth is, every time I saw my Uncle Lester alive he was on the couch, and he didn't look so different when he was dead. And then one day my Uncle Lester wasn't in the living room no more, and everyone said Aunt Margery buried him in the backyard. We didn't know for sure since no one was present at the burial, but there was a big patch of garden dug up. Aunt Margery always planted late-season cabbages there and they grew like the dickens."

Sharon and Cate didn't know what to say. They stared at Julie and their mouths dropped open slightly.

"I always felt a little funny eatin' them cabbages," Julie said as an afterthought.

Kellen moved behind Cate and put his hand on the small of her back. "Ladies," he said to Julie and Sharon.

"Howdy," Julie said.

Sharon nodded.

"The police are getting ready to clear out," Kellen said to Cate. "Is there anything you need to add to your statement?"

"No," Cate said. "I can't think of anything else."

"Would you like some company tonight?" Sharon asked Cate. "Julie and I could sleep over, so you wouldn't be alone up here. Or you could come down to my apartment."

"Thanks for the offer, but I'll be okay," Cate said. "I have Beast."

"Call if you change your mind," Sharon said.

Minutes later Kellen closed and locked the front door, and he and Cate stood for a moment appreciating the silence. The crime scene people were working in the stairwell, but everyone was out of the condo. A police strobe flashed against the living room window. The strobe originated from a lone squad car parked four floors below on the street. The strobe blinked off, and Cate sighed in relief. It was close to midnight.

"Are you really going to be okay alone in this condo tonight?" Kellen asked.

"Sure," Cate said. "I'll be fine." And she burst into tears.

Kellen gathered her to him and held her close, resting his head on hers.

"I don't know why I'm crying," Cate sobbed. "I didn't even know that dead guy. And nothing's missing or broken in Marty's condo. And I'm really pretty safe when I throw the bolt from the inside, right?"

"Right," Kellen said.

"Why am I blubbering like this?"

"Emotion," Kellen said. "Sometimes it just has to come out. You held yourself together when we found the body and during the whole police investigation, and now you can relax and let the emotion escape. It's like a safety valve."

"Why aren't you crying?"

"I'm a big strong man. It would be unseemly for me to cry like a little girl."

"Will you cry when you're alone?"

"No. I've seen a lot worse than this."

Cate snuffled and hiccupped and went to

the kitchen in search of a tissue. She blew her nose and stared at the butcher-block knife holder on the granite countertop. The large carving knife was missing. She looked in the dishwasher. Not there. She looked in the silverware drawer and the junk drawer. Not there.

Cate went back to the living room where Kellen was straightening furniture. "The large carving knife is missing," Cate said.

Kellen looked over at her. "Are you sure?"

"Pretty sure. I looked in all the drawers, and I can't find it."

"The body in the stairwell didn't have any knife wounds."

Cate shrugged and did one of those hand gestures that said *I dunno*.

"It's late," Kellen said. "And we're both tired. I think we should go to bed and clean this up in the morning."

"I have to get the blood off the floor tonight."

"I hear you. Where do you keep the mop?"

"It's not your problem."

"It *is* my problem," Kellen said, wrapping

his arms around Cate. "I really like you. I mean, *really* like you."

"I like you too," Cate said. "But I'm not sure I trust you."

"Smart woman," Kellen said. And he brushed a kiss across her lips, and then he gave her a second kiss that lingered and deepened and turned very serious.

Cate felt the need curl into her, and she instinctively pressed herself against Kellen. His hand immediately moved to her butt, holding her in place.

"Oops," Cate said. "I didn't mean to do that."

"It's done," Kellen said. "You can't take it back."

"It was an accident."

"I liked it."

"I can tell," Cate said.

Kellen looked down at her. "Still too soon?"

"Yes."

"Okay, how about this . . . I clean your kitchen floor, and you go to bed. When I'm done I'll sleep in Marty's room. Tomorrow morning I'll buy you breakfast, and we can talk."

"That would be really nice of you. I wasn't looking forward to dealing with the blood. I'll owe you."

"I'm counting on it," Kellen said.

Kellen was on the couch, text-messaging on his BlackBerry when Cate emerged from her bedroom with Beast.

"Did you sleep okay?" Cate asked Kellen.

"Yes. And I had a chance to comb through the condo again. And again, I found nothing. Marty steals expensive jewelry. He needs to keep it someplace until he moves it out to a fence. There's no safe here. Not even a strong-box. Where does Marty keep the jewelry?"

"He keeps his personal jewelry in the top drawer of his dresser. I've never seen any other jewelry in the condo. Maybe he uses a safety deposit box at his bank."

"I've been through his records. I can't find any evidence of a safety deposit box. No receipt. No reference to one. That doesn't mean one doesn't exist, but usually someone as organized as Marty keeps paperwork on file.

"The only item of interest that I found in my search is a key. One single key on a gold key chain. It looks like a house key. Does Marty have a partner?"

"You mean like a boyfriend? I don't think so."

"He never brought anyone home?"

"No. I'm sure he has friends, but he never brought anyone here. Maybe Marty has a second condo."

"If he does it isn't under his name. I've checked tax records."

"Beast and I are going walking," Cate said. "We'll be back in a half hour. You promised to take us to breakfast."

"We can do both simultaneously," Kellen said. "I'll walk Beast with you, and we can eat breakfast burgers in the park."

It was a little after eight in the morning and traffic was moving on Cate's street when they all trooped out. Sometime during the night it had rained, and the air felt scrubbed fresh of grime and toxins. Beast pranced in the cooler air and did what he had to do in the park. Kellen carted cartons of coffee and bags of egg-and-sausage burgers to a bench.

"I love this," Cate said, feeding a burger to Beast. "It's a morning picnic."

"I'd love it better if I felt I could keep you safe," Kellen said. "I don't like people breaking into your condo."

"One of the people who broke in isn't going to break in any more."

"True. But there were at least two people in your kitchen. I have a friend who's a locksmith. I'm going to send him over later this morning to change your front door lock."

"I can't do that. It isn't my condo. And Marty won't have a key."

"If Marty wants to get in he can ring the doorbell. And if you aren't home he can call you. I'm sure he has your cell number."

"I just assumed someone was picking the lock."

"It's possible, but it could also have been someone who had a key. You live in a secure building. The only way to get through the outside door is to get buzzed in by a tenant or to unlock the door with a key fob."

Cate finished her coffee and breakfast sandwich, and gave one last sandwich to Beast. They gathered the wrappers and bags and cups, tossed them all in the trash, and crossed the street. They were in front of the condo building when Kitty Bergman screeched to a stop and parked her Mercedes in a no-parking zone.

Kitty jumped out of her car and stormed over to Cate, waving a copy of the morning paper. Beast yelped and hid behind Kellen.

"What the heck is this about?" Kitty yelled. "Marty's agent found dead in the stairwell! Preliminary investigation suggests he fell down the stairs and broke his neck. First of all, I know Marty's agent, and that sack of horse manure would never use the stairs. And second, you killed him, didn't you?"

"Why would I want to kill him?"

"Everyone wanted to kill him. He was a disgusting parasite."

"I didn't know him," Cate said. "And I wasn't in the building when it happened."

"She was with me," Kellen said.

"Who are you?" Kitty asked.

"Kellen Koster."

Kitty hiked her Prada tote higher on her shoulder and narrowed her eyes at Kellen. "Is that supposed to mean something to me?"

"Not today, but maybe someday."

"Spare me the riddles," Kitty said. "I wouldn't be talking to you at all, but you look like you have a good package."

Cate and Kitty and Kellen studied his package for a moment.

"Thanks," Kellen finally said, smiling.

The elevator door opened, and Cate stepped in and pulled Beast in after her.

"Nice meeting you," Kellen said to Kitty. He followed Cate and Beast into the elevator and hit the button for the fourth floor. "Obviously a woman with keen powers of observation," Kellen said to Cate.

Chapter
TEN

Cate and Julie stared at Cate's kitchen counter. It was filled with cakes.

"Honey, that's a lot of cakes. Did you bake them all today?" Julie asked.

"Yep."

"What are you going to do with them?"

Cate didn't know. She'd already given cakes to everyone she could think of. "I wish school would start," Cate said. "I need something to occupy my mind. I don't start my shift at the bar until five tonight. That's two hours away."

"How about a pedicure?"

"Just did that."

"Oh, yeah," Julie said, looking down at Cate's toes. "I love that pink color. They're real pretty."

"I cleaned the condo. I walked Beast. I balanced my checkbook. I went food shopping."

"I guess you're trying to keep your mind off the dead man," Julie said.

"Yeah," Cate said on a sigh.

Actually Cate was trying to keep her mind off Kellen. Now that Kitty had drawn attention to his package it was all Cate could think about.

"Did you read the article in the paper this morning?" Julie asked. "It said the man's name was Irwin Moss. And it said he was Marty's agent. And the police thought Irwin came over to talk to Marty, and there was a fight, and Irwin left in a huff and fell down the stairs. And the police said they couldn't locate Marty. And they mentioned your name. They said you were Marty's housekeeper."

The phone rang and Cate got it in the kitchen.

"I'm in front of 2B again," Sharon said. "And I've got him this time. I know this will work. You have to come down to see."

"Now?" Cate asked.

"Now! Right now."

Cate and Julie stuck their heads out of the elevator when it opened on the second floor. They looked down the hall at Sharon, who was making giant *come here* signals to them, and they both stifled a grimace.

"Here's the deal," Sharon said. "I think he's in there. I've been watching all day. And I heard music playing around one o'clock. So I've got a couple packs of cigarettes, and we'll all light up and blow the smoke under his door. Eventually he'll see the smoke and rush out, and I'll have him!"

"Sweetie, you've been workin' too hard," Julie said. "Even *I* know that's a lame idea. And I'm not real smart."

"It's driving me nuts," Sharon said. "I know almost everyone in this building except *this* guy. What is he, a vampire? He never friggin' comes out during the day. I watch

every morning. And he never friggin' leaves."
Sharon turned to Julie. "Have you ever seen
him? You're always at the window. You'd see
him if he sneaked out, right?"

"I don't think I've seen him," Julie said.
"But there's always strange people comin'
and goin'. There's service people and visi-
tors. There's dog walkers and real estate people. And I'm not always at the window.
There's times when I go to the bathroom or I
make myself a sandwich."

"I have to start watching at night. That's
the solution to the problem," Sharon said. "I
could unroll a sleeping bag in front of his
door, and he'd have to step over me when he
came out."

"Maybe he travels a lot, like Marty," Julie
said. "Maybe there's no one in there, hardly
ever."

"I heard music," Sharon said. "Someone's
in there playing music!"

"I'm curious about 2B, but I'm not obsessed like you are," Cate said. "This is so
unlike you. You're the woman in charge of
her own destiny. You're the kick-ass realtor.
Why are you so hung up on this?"

"I don't know. I have this feeling. And it won't go away. It's as if something bad will happen if I don't find out who's living in 2B."

"It could be one of them karma things," Julie said. "Like you and 2B are star-crossed lovers. My cousin Lily once had a feeling like that. There was a boy got hired at the chicken processin' plant where Lily was workin', and the minute Lily saw him she knew he was the one. Trouble was, Lily was working the line in packaging, and this here guy was way down the line where they grind up the beaks and butts for dog food. And every day Lily would try to find a way to walk past this guy in beaks and butts. Lily just knew she was destined to meet him." Julie looked at her watch. "I should be goin'. I got an early trolley run tonight. Seniors group. We gotta get them back to the old people's home by nine."

"But what about Lily?" Sharon wanted to know. "Did she meet the beaks-and-butts guy?"

"Nope. Lily never did meet him. He just disappeared one day. And Lily married cousin Butch."

"Lily married her cousin?" Sharon asked.

"Well he wasn't her first cousin. And their kids turned out pretty normal, except for the youngest with the real bad crossed eyes."

"Go to the office and try to sell a house," Cate said to Sharon. "Julie and I will try to think of a way for you to meet 2B."

Sharon was holding four packs of cigarettes. "Are you sure the smoke is a bad idea?"

"Yes," Cate said. "Bad idea. Selling a house is a good idea."

Cate and Julie locked arms with Sharon and walked her into the elevator. Cate pushed the lobby button, and when the doors opened Cate and Julie walked Sharon out of the building.

"Go!" Cate said. "Be a realtor."

"If you want I could take a couple of your cakes and give them to the old folks on the trolley tonight," Julie said to Cate.

Cate was always caught by surprise when she entered Julie's apartment. She knew ahead of time what to expect, but the reality of the bare apartment was always shocking.

"I can see you're surprised," Julie said, carrying two cakes into the kitchen. "I guess you noticed right away that I got a new piece of furniture."

The new addition was a fold-up chaise longue with aluminum tubing and plastic webbing. It had taken the lawn chair's place in front of the television, and the lawn chair was now permanently in front of the window.

Cate followed Julie with more cakes. "You mean the chaise longue?"

"Yeah. We were going down the street in the trolley, and there it was, sitting out next to a Dumpster. So Fred stopped the trolley, and we folded the little devil up, and I took it home. It's real comfy. I can even recline when I watch television if I want."

Cate set her cakes on the counter next to Julie's. "It's nice of you to take these cakes. I hate to see them without a home."

"Sorry everything's such a mess," Julie said. "I got papers everywhere. I'm not much of an organizer."

Cate looked at the assortment of pads and loose pages on the counter. They were all filled with writing. "What is this?" Cate asked. "This looks like your handwriting."

"It's my observations. It's what I do all day until trolley time. And sometimes I come home and write at night, except it's hard on account of I only have one lamp."

Cate read one of the loose pages. It was about Julie going out on a date and coming home with her panties in her pocket and having them fall out when she was crossing Newbury Street. An elderly man had stopped traffic and retrieved Julie's panties, and as luck would have it, the party trolley had been first in line for the spectacle. Everyone on the trolley applauded, Julie took a bow and thanked the man who rescued her panties. The next day Julie applied for a job with the trolley and was instantly hired.

Cate read two more pages and thumbed through one of the pads. "Julie, this is good. It's funny and heartwarming and real. And it sounds just like you. It's engaging. You should do something with all these pages. Make a book or something."

"I thought of that," Julie said, "but I don't know where to begin. I think I'm good at writing things down but no good at putting them together."

"I have a lot of free time this week," Cate said. "I could type these into my computer and print them up for you. Maybe I can help organize."

"Wow, that would be so great," Julie said. "But only now when you have free time. I don't want to take up any time when you got classes. It's wonderful that you're gonna be a teacher."

Cate stacked the pads and looked at the loose pages that were scattered everywhere.

"I have a system," Julie said, collecting pages. "The crumples are throwaways."

Pugg was pacing outside the condo building when Cate flew out the door and hit the ground running, late for work.

"Pugg's been worried about you," Pugg said. "Pugg read about the dead man in the paper this morning. Shocking news. Pugg is dismayed. Pugg thinks he might have sold the man tires. Steel-belted."

"Were you out here last night, waiting for me?"

"No. Pugg had to work late last night. Pugg went to the bar, but you weren't there."

"I had the night off."

"Pugg found that out. Pugg went to the condo to see you, but couldn't get in. Everyone gets in but Pugg. Pugg saw the dead man go in."

Cate stopped short and stared at Pugg. "What?"

"Pugg saw the dead man go into the building. He got buzzed in. Pugg knows this because there was a picture of him in the paper."

"Do you know who buzzed him in?"

"No. Pugg was afraid it might have been you."

"It wasn't me. Was the man alone?"

"Yes. Pugg saw the man walk down the street. He was definitely alone."

"Do you remember the time?"

"It was seven thirty. Pugg tried to go in with the man, but Pugg was rebuffed. Pugg thinks the man might have remembered that Pugg jacked the price up a tad on the man's tires."

"Do you remember anyone else going into the building?"

"A very beautiful, very tall woman. Looked a little like a giant Judy Garland. If Pugg hadn't already promised himself to you, Pugg would have pursued her."

"The giant Judy Garland sounds familiar," Cate said. "And she's a man."

"Pugg is sure you're mistaken. Pugg came close to growing wood for her. Pugg would be very upset to learn he almost grew wood for a man."

"Did the woman arrive before the dead man?"

"Yes. She came in a town car, and she had one of those gizmos that opens the door."

"Did you see her leave?"

"No. Pugg went home after the dead man said he'd call the police on Pugg if Pugg kept trying to get into the building."

Tending bar can be a lot like driving a car, Cate thought. Without even realizing, sometimes you switch to autopilot, and next thing you know, you're in your garage, and you can't remember how you got there. Cate was working on autopilot tonight, moving from one end of the bar to the other, filling orders, making conversation, and the whole time she was reviewing facts about Marty. If he was back in town (and Cate was pretty sure he was) where was he staying and what role did he play in Irwin's death? And what was the deal with the missing knife?

Cate gave a small squeak of surprise when a hand clamped onto her wrist.

"Earth to Cate," Kellen said. "You just gave me a glass of Chardonnay. And it's got two olives in it."

"Wasn't thinking." Cate swapped the wine out for beer. "I have a lot on my mind."

"Anything you want to share?"

Cate told him about her conversation with Pugg.

"Not a lot of giant Judy Garlands walking around these days," Kellen said.

"Assuming Marty has returned, what will you do?"

"I'll stick close to you. You're living in his condo. He came back once. I'm betting he'll come back again. And he can't get in without you. You have the new lock."

"I thought you had the lock changed for my safety."

"That too," Kellen said.

"If Marty is a master thief I'm guessing he's also good with locks."

"He'll have a hard time with this lock. He'll have to use a computer. And I doubt he has what he'll need. From what I've been able to determine, Marty can open a door, but not a safe. Marty is an opportunist. He looks for a necklace left on the bathroom vanity or a safe left unlocked. It's one of the reasons he's survived. He takes things that are available to anyone walking into the room . . . a waitress with the caterer, a guest, a member of the household staff. And Marty's hits are spread all over the country, so no one saw a pattern. No one suspected a professional thief."

"Until you."

"Almost a year ago I was hired to find a pair of earrings that were stolen from a house in upstate New York. They were taken during a party, and I investigated everyone attending. Marty was one of the names on the list. He performed. My present client had a necklace taken during a charity event, and the first thing that jumped out at me was

Marty's name on the attending list. I was able to get a work history on him for the past two years and discovered there was an unusual number of thefts associated with his appearances."

"Can you make enough money stealing the occasional necklace to make the risk worthwhile?"

"I came up with seventeen thefts in two years. And I probably didn't find everything. Of those seventeen hits only six were worth less than a hundred thousand dollars. In most cases there were multiple pieces taken, plus cash on hand. Three hits went seven digits. Marty wouldn't get full value for any of the pieces, but he'd do okay. He'd make more than enough to buy his new Porsche plus the art in his condo."

Cate made a bar run, refilling drinks, cashing out customers. She returned to Kellen and swapped out his empty bowl of bar nuts for a fresh one. "Do you know what happens to the jewelry when it leaves Marty's hands?"

"No, but I'm pretty sure he doesn't get rid

of it locally. I suspect the larger pieces might go out of the country."

"Wouldn't that be complicated? Security checks at airports and whatever."

"TSA looks for bombs, not necklaces," Kellen said. "And the fence probably takes possession in this country but shops the stones, if not the whole piece, in Europe or South America."

"I thought I had a safe living arrangement until I finished school and got a job teaching. Now I find out I'm living with a thief. Do you think Marty's dangerous?"

"Under ordinary circumstances, no. Under stress, maybe. Marty is supposed to perform here tomorrow night. Do you know if he's canceled?"

"I asked Evian," Cate said. "He hasn't canceled."

"If Marty is performing there's a real good chance he'll return to the condo tonight or tomorrow. He's got clothes and makeup there."

"Thinking about it gives me an upset stomach. I'm the world's worst actress. I'm no good at fibbing. He's going to know something's weird. And it's not like I can avoid speaking to him. His agent died in our stairwell last night. That requires mention. And here's the worst part . . . I can't stand the thought of giving up Beast. He sleeps on my bed with me. And he's cuddly. And he's a good listener. And I think he likes me."

Kellen blew out a sigh. "I wish that was a description of me."

"I'm worried Marty's going to come back, and he's going to take Beast." A tear popped out and slid down Cate's cheek. "Shit," she said.

Kellen wiped the tear away with his fingertip. It was official. He was in love with Cate Madigan. He didn't care what he had to do, but he was going to make things right. And no matter what, Cate wasn't going to lose her Beast. "We'll make it all work out."

"We?"

"Yeah. You and me. We're a team, right?"

"Maybe," Cate said. "I'm not sure how much I trust you."

"Are we talking about professional ethics or about sex?" Kellen asked.

"Both."

"That's easy. My business ethics are beyond question. And when it comes to sex, you can't trust me at all. I want you bad."

"Good grief."

Chapter
ELEVEN

"This is *not* a good idea," Cate said.

"Do you have a better one?" Kellen asked.

"No."

"Then I'm staying. We'll stop at my place, so I can pick up some clothes, and I'll move in with you and Beast for a couple days." It was a little after eleven, and Kellen was holding hands with Cate, gently tugging her past her condo building. "I'm only a couple blocks away."

"What will I tell Marty if he comes home?"

"You'll tell him you love me more than life itself and can't bear to be separated from me."

"That's why you're sleeping on the couch?"

"I won't be sleeping on the couch. I'll be in bed with you, acting like I have self-control."

Yes, but what about me? Cate thought. What if *I* don't have any self-control?

Kellen stopped at a brownstone and plugged his key into the door.

"This is a whole house," Cate said. "Three floors. On one of the nicest streets in the South End."

"I'm good at my job," Kellen said. "I get paid well for looking, and I get paid even better for finding. This is a little bare. I just closed on it last month, and I haven't had much time for interior decorating."

The front door opened to a small foyer. Living room to the left. Dining room to the right. Stairs with a graceful wood banister led to the second floor. Floors were polished mahogany. Kellen had a large flat-screen television hung over the elaborate fireplace in the living room. An Oriental rug had been placed in front of the fireplace, and a large glass coffee table and comfy leather couch sat on the rug, facing the television. The dining room was unfurnished.

"I'll only be a minute," Kellen said. "Make yourself at home while I go upstairs and throw a few things into a gym bag."

Cate prowled through the dining room and into the kitchen. It was twice the size of Marty's condo kitchen, with new granite countertops and stainless-steel appliances. It looked completely untouched. Pristine oven. No splatters on the cooktop. Over the counter, cabinets were empty. No dishes. No glasses. No silverware. She looked in the side-by-side refrigerator. Beer, orange juice, bread, peanut butter. There was a butter knife in the refrigerator alongside the peanut butter.

Kellen came into the kitchen carrying his gym bag. "It turns out I'm not especially domestic," he said. "I'd like this place to look like a home with cookies and a coffeemaker and a drawer filled with clean socks, but

I don't know where to begin. I've been building my business, living on the road wherever the job took me for so long, I only own one butter knife."

"Will you have a chance to spend any amount of time here?"

"Yes. My business is changing. I'm now able to do all the preliminary investigation by computer and phone from the office upstairs. And I have two investigators who do the legwork. So hopefully my days on the road are a thing of the past. Or at least they'll be limited."

"It's a really nice house. And it's a great kitchen."

Kellen had a flash of insight regarding his house's missing ingredient. It wasn't cookies and a coffeemaker that were going to make this house a home. It was a redheaded woman and a big, sloppy dog.

Ten minutes later Cate and Kellen were back in front of Marty's condo building. Pugg was there too, holding a bloody handkerchief to his nose.

"What happened?" Cate wanted to know.

"Pugg was at the record store at the end of Newbury Street, and Pugg saw the giant Judy Garland leaving the store. So Pugg followed at a discreet distance. Pugg was curious to see if Judy exhibited any manly traits. Pugg followed Judy for several blocks, and then Judy crossed to Commonwealth. And Pugg still followed. Pugg's observation to this point was that Judy was a lady in every sense of the word. Her clothes were very tasteful, and she had a very ladylike walk."

"Judy Garland?" Kellen asked.

"Marty," Cate said.

Pugg pressed his lips together at the suggestion that Judy's name might be Marty. "Anyway, *Judy* stopped at a townhouse and took her key out to open her front door and suddenly this terrible blond woman jumped out of the bushes. She said she knew Judy would show up. And she said she knew Judy hadn't taken care of business. And Judy was quite startled. Pugg could tell Judy was no match for this blond woman, so Pugg stepped in. 'Excuse me,' Pugg said to Judy. 'Do you require some assistance?' And this blond woman told Pugg to butt out and punched Pugg in the nose."

"And did you butt out?" Kellen asked.

"Yes. Pugg was bleeding profusely. And Pugg noticed there were two large men standing in the shadows on the side of the house. Pugg thinks they were with the blond woman."

"So you abandoned Judy?" Cate asked.

"Like a rat on a sinking ship," Pugg said. "But Pugg called the police on his cell phone. And then Pugg came here to tell you. Your name isn't on the list of occupants, but Pugg was prepared to buzz everyone until he found you."

"Pugg is disturbingly tenacious," Cate said.

"Fucking A," Pugg said.

Julie's head popped out of her window. "Hey y'all, what's goin' on down there? Are you talkin' to that adorable, furry little guy?"

"Would you be referring to Pugg?" Pugg asked.

"I don't know," Julie said. "What's a Pugg?"

"I'm a Pugg," he said.

"I thought Pugg was a little dawg," Julie

said. "Why have you got that handkerchief to your nose?"

"Pugg was injured trying to help a lady in distress."

"You poor thing," Julie said. "You come on up here, and I'll put some ice on it. Just go to the door, and I'll buzz you in, sweetie."

Pugg turned to Cate. "Pugg hopes you'll understand if he gives you the kiss-off. Pugg thinks he has a chance to score with the window lady."

Cate and Kellen followed Pugg to Julie's apartment.

"I can't recommend this guy," Cate said to Julie. "He's actually toe fungus."

"Maybe he's just a diamond in the rough," Julie said. "And it must be hard bein' a Pugg. Is that some foreign country?" Julie asked Pugg.

"Pugg is a name. Patrick Pugg. Pugg doesn't believe in the use of 'I.' Pugg always refers to himself as Pugg."

"That could get wearin' on a person," Julie said.

"Nonsense," Pugg said. "Pugg is charming. Pugg is adorable."

"Pugg better stop talkin' like that or I'm gonna push his nuts so far up his hairy little body they're gonna come out his nose," Julie said.

"That would be uncomfortable," Pugg said.

Julie had a wet towel pressed to Pugg's face. "My Uncle Lester got kicked in the nuts one time, and it turned his hair white all over his body. He became one of them albinos," she said. "I didn't see him when he got kicked, but I saw him when he was white, and it was something. It was shortly after that he got a job with a chemical plant and fell in a vat of formaldehyde. Lester was one of those people, if they didn't have bad luck they wouldn't have any luck at all."

"What happened to Lester?" Pugg wanted to know.

"Oddly enough he didn't die," Julie said. "But he was always strange after that. And the formaldehyde smell never went away. You always knew when Uncle Lester was in the room. It was like being in biology lab when they opened the jars of pickled frogs."

"That's a very weird story," Pugg said.

"Not in my hometown," Julie said. "We got a bunch of people born downwind of the nuclear power plant and there's some tales to be told on those folks."

"Did you get the address on the townhouse on Commonwealth?" Kellen asked Pugg.

"Pugg didn't . . . oops!" Pugg clapped his hands over his privates. "Pugg means *I*! *I* didn't get the number, but *I* know the house. It's on the block between Gloucester and Hereford. On the side of the street toward Prudential Center. And it's easy to find because it has a red door."

Kellen took a step back and looked at the townhouse in front of him. Four stories if you counted the garden level. Classic brownstone. Newly restored. All windows were dark at one o'clock in the morning. The house was on Commonwealth Avenue between Gloucester and Hereford Streets. It had a red door. Kellen reached into his pocket and removed Marty's key. He plugged it into the big brass lock on the front door, and nothing happened. He turned and looked at Cate and shrugged.

Cate was ten feet back, on the sidewalk, doing lookout for Kellen, and she was thinking he seemed disturbingly comfortable attempting the task of breaking and entering. In fact he was comfortable with a whole bunch of skills Cate ordinarily would find alarming in a man, not the least of which was lying. Kellen McBride-Koster was hands down the best liar Cate had ever met. And yet, Cate was increasingly attracted to him. He was charming and confident and smart. And he was willing to step up and be a hero if a hero was needed.

He was standing in a splash of moonlight, and Cate thought he was flat out sexy in dark jeans and a button-down black shirt with the sleeves rolled to his elbows. Her mother's words echoed in her head, *too easy on the eyes, hard on the heart*. And then Julie's words echoed in her head, *take him out for a test drive*. Cate chewed on her lower lip. She was leaning toward Julie's words.

"It's hard to tell for sure from here, but it looks to me like the house two doors down also has a red door," Cate softly called to Kellen.

Kellen silently moved from the stoop to Cate's side and looked down the street. "I guess red is a popular color for doors."

Kellen had no luck with the second door he tried, but the lock tumbled on the door to the third house. The third red door belonged to one of the smaller houses on the block. The house was in deep shadow, receiving little light from the gaslight-type streetlight at the curb, and only scattered moonlight filtered through the shade tree in the minuscule front yard.

"Okay, so we know this is the house," Cate said. "Now what?"

"Now we hope he isn't home," Kellen said. And he put his finger on the doorbell and pushed. "He doesn't know me. If he answers the door I can pretend to be drunk and lost. I suggest *you* hide in the bushes."

Cate scooted close to the building, crouched behind an azalea, and held her breath.

Kellen rang the bell again. And again.

"Nobody home," Kellen said. He opened the door and stepped inside, motioning Cate to follow.

Cate scrambled out of the bush and into

the house. She stood in the dark foyer and listened to something beeping. "What's that?" Cate asked.

"Alarm," Kellen said, taking her hand. "It's ready to go off. Don't get scared. It's going to be noisy."

The alarm started to wail, and Kellen wrapped his arms around Cate and held her close. He had his mouth to her ear.

"I can feel your heart racing," he said.

"The police are going to come in and take us to jail."

"Probably not. They'll try the front and back doors and find them locked. They'll shine their flashlights in the windows and see that everything is okay and that there are no signs of forced entry. And they'll leave. The alarm company will alert someone, most likely Marty, but it'll be a while before he'll arrive to check things out. If ever. We'll be gone by then."

"You've done this before."

"Nothing I'd admit to.

Somewhere in the house a phone was ringing.

"That's the alarm company," Kellen said.

"When no one answers they'll send the police." He opened the coat closet door and pushed Cate in. "Stay here and keep the door closed until I come for you. I can go through the house faster if I'm alone."

There were two coats hanging in the closet, and Cate recognized Marty's cologne on them. This was his house, and they'd broken into it. Okay, so they had a key, but they'd sort of stolen the key. She slipped behind the coats and tried to stay calm. Her heart was still banging in her chest. I'm not cut out for this, she thought. I never wanted to be James Bond. I always wanted to be Mr. Rogers. The phone was no longer ringing, but the alarm continued to wail. It was pitch-black in the closet. Too dark for Cate to read the dial on her watch. And then the alarm stopped and the silence was crushing.

Cate took shallow breaths and listened. She could hear someone try the front door. Her heart was stuck in her throat. She was going to throw up and faint, she thought. And when she regained consciousness she was never going to talk to Kellen again. What the heck was he thinking? Normal people just didn't do this stuff. This was burglar stuff. This was *crazy*.

The door rattling stopped and Cate stayed statue still. She felt her pulse normalize a little, and she slumped against the closet wall and waited. And then without warning the alarm came back on. She heard footsteps on the stairs, the closet door was yanked open, and Kellen reached in for her.

"We're leaving," Kellen said. "We're going to use the kitchen door. It'll let us out into the alley behind the house."

"It's totally black in here. How can you see?"

"Penlight," Kellen said, flicking his hand.

Cate looked down and saw the point of light on the floor. She was so scared she hadn't picked it up on her own.

Kellen tugged her down the center hall, quickly moving her through the house. They were in the kitchen, out the kitchen door, crossing a small enclosed patio, out the patio door, and standing in a one-lane, very dark alley that ran behind all the houses. They were two houses from Gloucester Street. Cate could see the streetlight at the end of the alley. Kellen still had her hand, pulling her along. He broke into a run. They were in sneakers, and they made almost no noise as they ran for Gloucester. They crossed the street at Gloucester and headed for Prudential Center and, beyond that, the South End.

They'd just reached Boylston when Cate saw the police cruiser. It was moving toward them fast, lights flashing, no siren. Kellen stepped into the shadow of a doorway and pulled Cate hard against him. He kissed her, and the cruiser slowed but didn't stop as it rolled past. Not the world's most romantic kiss, both of them with eyes wide open, watching the cruiser.

"I'd like to stay and do a better job of kissing you," Kellen said, "but we need to keep moving."

"What happened back there?"

Kellen silently cursed himself for not being more careful and endangering Cate. "The alarm reset itself, and I tripped the motion sensors. It would have been nice to have a little more time, but I found out what I needed to know."

They were walking down Boylston, holding

hands and talking, looking like a couple on their way home from a late date. They turned at Dartmouth and walked toward Columbus and Tremont, and Cate finally began to relax.

"Marty has been using the house," Kellen said, "but I think it's a stopover, as opposed to a second home. I didn't see any expensive artwork, and the furniture doesn't reflect Marty's taste. He has some clothes there, but not a lot. Bare essentials in the bathroom. No condoms that I could see, so I'm guessing he doesn't use the house for fun. It didn't seem like he shared it with anyone. Nothing in the refrigerator. There was a wall safe upstairs, but it was open and empty. He had a suitcase on the bed. It was partially unpacked. I think Marty was snatched, and so far hasn't been returned."

"Snatched by Kitty Bergman?"

"That's my best guess. And I bet when I check the tax records I find Bergman owns that townhouse."

"I don't get it. I don't understand any of this. What on earth is Kitty Bergman's involvement? She's rich, and she's a social powerhouse. I knew she and Marty were friends, but I thought they just shopped for dresses together."

"Maybe charity is boring."

"Do you think we should try to rescue Marty?"

"I'm not in rescue. I'm in retrieval. Marty's on his own . . . at least for tonight."

Chapter
TWELVE

Kellen was hands on hips in an oversized gray T-shirt and navy boxers. The boxers looked new and had little green-and-yellow palm trees on them. "What the heck are you wearing?" he asked Cate. "You look like you're ready for Alaska."

They were standing beside Cate's bed, and Cate was wearing socks and sweatpants and a hooded sweatshirt. The twenty-first-century equivalent to a chastity belt.

"This is what I wear to bed," Cate said. In January. And when I'm sleeping with a man I'm not ready to sleep with.

Kellen grinned. "You can run, but you can't hide."

"What's that supposed to mean?"

Kellen slipped under the covers. "It means you can avoid a relationship with me for a while but eventually I'm going to win."

Kellen didn't want to alarm Cate, but after an evening of breaking and entering, dinner with her family, and a morning picnic where he watched her feed her giant dog breakfast sandwiches, Kellen was having thoughts of happily ever after. Yes, sir, Kellen thought, he wasn't just going for the sheet time. He wanted the whole enchilada. Kellen was thinking marriage. How weird was that?

The air-conditioning was on, but Cate was starting to sweat. And it wasn't sweat from passion. Cate was sweating from fleece.

"Tell me again why you have to sleep in *my* bed."

"I tried sleeping on the leather couch but

it was too slippery. I kept sliding off. And we agreed that I shouldn't sleep in Marty's room again because if he figured it out he wouldn't think we were a couple. And the truth is, that's all a lot of bullshit. I'm in your bed because I want to be in your bed."

"Whatever," Cate said, "but you're on my side. Could you at least move over?"

"I can't move over. Your dog is sleeping there."

Beast was stretched out with his head on the pillow, sound asleep. Cate tried to roll him to the edge, and he opened an eye and growled.

"He didn't mean that in a threatening way," Cate said.

"Uh-huh."

"*Beast,*" Cate said in his ear. "Wake up. You have to move over."

Beast half opened his eyes.

"Poor baby is sleepy," Cate said.

"I'm sleepy too," Kellen said. "I wish you would get into bed."

"Okay, fine, perfect!" Cate said. And she climbed over Kellen and wedged herself in between him and Beast.

"Comfy?" Kellen asked.

"Yes. And you?"

"Yep." And he turned the light off.

Truth was, Cate wasn't comfy. Cate was roasting. Sweat was rolling down the side of her face. She tried to move to find some cool sheet but there was no open space.

"Now what?" Kellen said.

"Excuse me?"

"You're thrashing around like a fish out of water."

"I'm trapped in here. I can't breathe."

Kellen turned the light on and looked at her. "You can't breathe because you're in this stupid sweat suit. What have you got under it?"

"Tank top and underwear." Actually the underwear was a pink lace thong, but she thought it best not to share that information with Kellen.

"This is ridiculous. You look like you're going to have heat stroke," Kellen said. He grabbed the sweatshirt by the bottom ribbing and in two seconds it was over Cate's head and lying on the floor. "Better?" he asked.

"Yes, but . . ."

"Now get rid of the socks and the sweat-pants."

"No way!"

"Do I have to wrestle you out of them?"

"Good grief," Cate said, shucking the sweatpants and socks. "How did I get myself into this dilemma?"

"For starters, you chose the wrong room-mate."

"He seemed like such a nice guy."

"Just because he steals jewelry doesn't mean he isn't a nice guy."

Cate settled in between Kellen and Beast, Kellen turned the light off for the second time, and everyone lay motionless and rigid for two minutes. Finally Kellen blew out a sigh.

"This bed is too small," he said. "Now you've got everything pressed against me."

"And?"

"And you're all smooth and silky and warm and soft. And I'm *really* uncomfortable."

"It wasn't *my* idea to sleep in the same bed. And it wasn't *my* idea to remove the sweat suit."

"Okay, how about this. How about if we get engaged."

"Engaged? Are you insane? I hardly know you."

"Honey, in a couple minutes you're going to know me pretty well."

"Have you ever been married?" Cate asked.

"No."

"Do you have any children?"

"No."

"Diseases?"

"No. And I've got all my teeth. I don't have a criminal record. And my cholesterol is perfect."

"All good things to know," Cate said. "How do you stand on the flat tax?"

"Oh hell," Kellen said, turning to Cate, draping his leg over hers, and wrapping her in his arms.

"And what about birth control?" she asked him.

"I've got it covered," Kellen said.

Cate slid her hand down Kellen's flat stomach, her thumb dipping into the waistband of his boxers, and a nervous giggle escaped from her lips. It seemed like a lot to cover.

Kellen moved against her, and his hands found their way under her T-shirt, skimming over places that were soft and sensitive, his mouth following close behind his fingertips. He slid his hand under the little pink satin thong, sliding it down Cate's legs, over her perfect feet, and onto the floor at the end of the bed.

Beast's head shot up and within half a second he was on the floor, pink thong in mouth.

All romantic activity stopped dead, and Cate sat up and gaped at Beast, frozen in horror. There was a little strap of elastic band hanging out from his lips like dental floss.

Kellen pointed at Beast. "Drop it!"

Gulp. Gone.

"He ate my underwear! My favorite thong. What do we do now? He might choke. Do you know the Heimlich maneuver? Should we take him to a vet? Does the Angell Memorial Hospital send ambulances?"

"Don't worry. He'll be fine. I sympathize with the favorite thong part, but that scrap of fabric you call underwear was hardly enough to choke a hundred-twenty-pound dog. It was barely a snack."

Cate thought about the path her panties would be taking, and that it was probably best to let them go.

"At least Beast is out of the bed now." Kellen's Big Bad Wolf smile had returned. "I needed more room to do my best work."

His fingers magically found the most sensitive of Cate's sensitive spots, and all of her worries were temporarily washed away. Clearly this was a man whose skills and knowledge went beyond those of breaking and entering and training dogs.

Cate stood in the shower and let the water beat on her. It was morning, and she was tired and a little sore in strange places, having used muscles last night that she hadn't used in a while. Well heck, if she was going to be completely honest, she'd probably used muscles she'd *never* used.

She shampooed her hair and wondered if she was engaged. She was almost positive Kellen hadn't been serious. And she was afraid to ask. She didn't know what she'd say to a real proposal. She was half afraid she'd say *yes*.

"Hey," Kellen called from the other side of the bathroom door. "I'm running late. Do you mind if I come in?"

Before Cate could answer, she had a big naked guy in the shower with her.

"I don't know if you're going to fit in here," she said.

"Yeah, you said that last night, but we made it work, right?"

Cate clapped a hand over her mouth to squelch a giggle.

"I forgot about a staff meeting," Kellen said, soaping up and rinsing off. He gave Cate a kiss and grabbed a towel. "I hope I didn't promise breakfast."

"I have a box of Pop-Tarts in the kitchen."

"That'll do," Kellen said. And he was out of the bathroom.

Cate wrapped herself in her terry robe and followed him out. "I have a huge favor to ask."

"Anything."

"I'm worried about Beast. I'm afraid Marty will come back and take Beast."

"Cate, I know you love Beast, but technically he's Marty's dog."

Not that it mattered to Kellen. If Cate wanted to keep Beast she was going to keep Beast, and Kellen knew he would do whatever was necessary to make it happen.

"He doesn't know Marty," Cate said. "And he's just a baby. And Marty is a thief. And maybe even a murderer. Suppose he pushed his agent down the stairs." Cate squeezed out a tear. "That's not the sort of man who should have a dog like Beast."

Kellen grinned. "You had to work hard to squeeze that tear out. You're manipulating me."

"Is it working?"

"Yep." He pulled on socks and laced up his sneakers. "Get a doggy bag together for me. Remember, I'm the guy with the great house and no food or dishes. I've got a full morning, and I think I have an early afternoon meeting, and then I'm free. Do you want me to keep Beast at my house, or do you want me to bring him back here tonight?"

"I want you to keep him at your house until things are settled."

Kellen wasn't an expert on fairy tales, but

he was pretty sure the knight in shining armor wasn't supposed to be guarding the distressed damsel's dragon.

Cate had Julie's pages everywhere . . . on the floor, on the dining room table, on the kitchen counters. She'd been working all morning at numbering them and putting them in order. While she'd been organizing she'd been reading. Julie was telling the story of a small-town girl struggling to find herself in a big city. She talked about her mama and her cousins and the pain and the excitement of leaving them. She talked about the people who passed under her window. She talked about being lonely and poor and feeling rich and being in love with life. She talked about her friends and her job on the trolley, and in some mysterious way it all was bound together into a story with a beginning and a middle and an end.

Cate thought it was amazing. Julie had written a book. And it was *good*. It had some rough edges but that was part of the charm. Just like it was part of Julie's charm. Scratch the surface of the down-home girl and you found a complex person with a surprising understanding of human nature. Easy to underestimate someone like Julie, Cate thought as she collected the pages. Julie walked and talked country, and Cate realized Julie sometimes used that image to her advantage. She even had a term for it. Country sneaky.

"Just 'cause you don't use big words, don't mean you're stupid," Cate said to the empty condo, adding the last couple of pages to her stack and securing it all with a giant rubber band.

The manuscript needed to go from Julie's scrawl to neatly typed pages, and probably there was a standard format writers used, Cate thought. And probably she could get the information online.

She made herself a peanut butter sandwich and leaned against the counter while she ate. She looked down at the floor. No Beast water bowl. She'd given it to Kellen, along with Beast's food and toys and vitamins and toothbrush and treats. The condo felt sterile without Beast. No snuffling, slobbering noises. No warm dog body pressing against her leg. Hard to believe Beast was delivered just three days ago. It felt like he'd always been part of her life. And what about Kellen? That relationship was four days old, and already Kellen had moved into her bed and her heart. How had that happened?

The doorbell rang and Cate had a moment of panic. On the one hand she wanted it to be Marty so she could get some answers. On the other hand she was dreading the charade.

She had both hands' fingers crossed on the way to the door. "Don't let it be Marty," she chanted. "Don't let it be Marty!"

She looked out the peephole and grimaced. There was good news and bad news. The good news was that Marty wasn't standing in the hall. The bad news was that Kitty Bergman was out there, backed up by two large men in dark suits.

Cate opened the door a crack. "Yes?" she said to Kitty.

"What's with the fancy lock?" Kitty wanted to know. "Do you think you have something to protect? Something to hide?"

Without waiting for an answer, Kitty pushed past Cate into the condo with the two men on her heels.

"If you're looking for Marty," Cate said, "he isn't here."

"I know he isn't here," Kitty said. "I just talked to him and he asked me to come get his dog."

Cate's heart gave a painful contraction. "Beast isn't here."

"Well, where is he?"

"He's visiting with a friend."

"Yeah, I almost believe that," Kitty said. She flicked her eyes to the two men. "Search for the dog. And bring his food and dog bowls."

"Why didn't Marty come to get his dog?" Cate asked.

"Marty's busy."

The two men returned to the living room.

"The dog isn't here," the one guy said. "And we couldn't find any dog things. No food or bowls or anything."

"Maybe you're not as dumb as you look," Kitty said to Cate.

"I didn't know I looked dumb," Cate said.

"Where's the dog?"

"I told you he's at a friend's house."

Kitty looked like she might lunge forward at any moment and grab Cate by the neck and start squeezing. "Does your friend have a name?"

"Yes," Cate said.

"Would you like to tell me your friend's name?"

"No," Cate said. "I don't feel comfortable with this. If Marty wants his dog he's going to have to show up in person."

"Are you suggesting you don't trust me with Marty's dog?" Kitty Bergman asked, eyes narrowed.

"I just don't understand why Marty isn't here. If he's in town, why didn't he come home?"

"I told you. He's busy. Now be a good girl and get the dog. I'm sure he's somewhere in the building. With the realtor? With Miss Party Trolley?"

"He's not with either of them."

"I'm losing patience," Kitty said. "I'm

going to count to five. If I'm not satisfied with the information I've received from you by the time I get to five, I'm going to walk out of this condo and leave you with my two friends. They can be very persuasive."

"I don't get it," Cate said. "Why is Beast so important? Marty's never even seen him."

"Yes," Kitty said. "But Marty's already emotionally attached. And as his friend I feel obligated to get him his dog."

One of the men wrapped his hand around Cate's arm. "Wait in the hall," he said to Kitty. "We'll take care of this."

Kitty Bergman opened the condo front door to go into the hall, and Julie and Patrick Pugg tumbled in.

"Thank you," Julie said. "We was out there wonderin' how we were gonna get through the lock. Cate told me how to do it, but I forgot."

Pugg looked to Julie. "Pugg is in hero mode now. Pugg needs to be Pugg. Pugg would like a temporary amnesty on nuts rearrangement."

"Amnesty granted," Julie said.

"Unhand her," Pugg said to the guy holding Cate's arm.

The guy smiled. "Who's gonna make me?"

"Pugg will make you. Pugg is no one to be trifled with," Pugg said.

"Haw!" the guy said. "That's a good one."

"This is silly," Cate said. "Let's not get all carried away."

"Oh for God's sake," Kitty said. "Can we please get on with this?" She pointed to goon number two. "You! Get rid of the fat bumpkin and the bridge troll."

"Excuse me," Julie said. "Are you referrin' to me? Because I am not *fat*. I'm *ample*. And I'm not goin' anywhere. You're the one who needs to be goin'. I think you've worn out your welcome here."

Kitty had taken a wide stance in her Louboutin slingbacks, and had a white-knuckle grip on her classic Chanel shoulder purse. "I told you to get rid of them," she snapped to goon number two. "Are you deaf? Are you an idiot? What are you waiting for?"

Goon number two reached for Julie, and Pugg jumped up and punched him in the nose. Since Pugg was a foot shorter than goon number two it wasn't much of a punch.

Goon number two looked down at Pugg. "What the heck do you think you're doing?"

"Pugg is protecting his women," Pugg said.

"I don't think so," the goon said. "I think you and bumpkin's gonna get removed, so we can have it nice and peaceful while we slap the redhead around."

"Pugg will be forced to punch you in the nose again unless you leave the premises this instant," Pugg said.

The goon blew out a sigh, like Pugg was being a trial. "Ms. Bergman," goon number two said, "would you please open the door for me?"

Kitty opened the door, and goon number two grabbed Pugg by the seat of his pants and threw him out the door, into the hall.

"Ow," Pugg said. "Pugg got a wedgie."

"I hope you aren't plannin' on doing that to me," Julie said to goon number two, "because that would be real rude."

"Guess I'm just a rude kind of guy," goon number two said, moving toward Julie.

Julie pulled a semiautomatic 9mm out of her shoulder bag and aimed it at goon number two's privates.

"Holy cow," Cate said. "Where'd you get a gun?"

"Where I come from everybody's got a gun." Julie looked at Cate. "Honey, don't you have a gun?"

"No."

"Well darn, that's part of your problem here. What do you think you got a peephole for? It's to see whether you need to answer the door with your gun in your hand."

"You won't use that gun," goon number two said.

"I can pick off a river rat at fifty paces," Julie said. "I wouldn't have any problem shootin' you in the wiener, however small and insignificant it might be. And you should be happy it's not my Aunt Tess standing here. Loogie Bayard got drunk and broke into Aunt Tess's house one night, and tried to have his way with her, and Aunt Tess took the meat mallet to him. He was a terrible mess. She even cracked his glass eye. Not that it was worth much. Loogie got it at the VA hospital, and it was always wanderin' around lookin' in the wrong direction."

Everyone stood for a moment digesting that information.

"You haven't heard the end of this," Kitty

said to Cate. "I want that dog." And Kitty turned on her heel and swished out of the condo with the two men close behind. Pugg, who was standing outside, edged his way back in.

Cate closed and locked the door after them and gave a small hysterical giggle. "Yikes."

"And double yikes," Julie said. "What was that about?"

"The dog," Cate said. "Kitty said Marty asked her to get the dog."

"That's a lot of baloney," Julie said. "That woman never did a favor for nobody. She wouldn't come fetchin' a dog for Marty. You told me they weren't even getting' along." Julie looked around. "Where is the big guy? Where's Beast?"

"I sent him home with Kellen."

"Lucky thing I was lookin' out the window when Kitty and the goon squad trooped into the building," Julie said. "I thought they looked like they were up to no good, so I sent Pugg to see where they were goin'. When he found out they were in with you, we came right away."

Pugg adjusted his underwear. "Pugg hopes

you don't mind," Pugg said to Cate, "but Pugg has transferred his affections to Julie. Julie came across."

"He'd be a keeper in my hometown," Julie said by way of explanation.

"Yes, but this is Boston!" Cate said.

"He has some good points," Julie said. "He's a real hard worker, if you know what I mean. And it's hard to tell for sure what's under all that fur, but I bet he'd clean up okay if you gave him a whole-body wax."

The doorbell rang again and everyone went raised eyebrows. The lock clicked, and Kellen pushed the door open.

"I needed a break, so I thought I'd stop in and say hello," Kellen said.

"Pugg needs to get back to work now that his job as hero is done," Pugg said.

"I'll walk you out," Julie said. "And don't you worry I'm gonna make sure nobody gives you a wedgie but me from now on."

"I have a feeling I missed something," Kellen said when Julie and Pugg had left.

"Kitty Bergman was here with two henchmen. She wanted Beast. She said Marty sent her."

"Kitty Bergman doing errands for Marty?"

"Yeah, that's what Julie said. Doesn't compute. Anyway, things were starting to get ugly until Julie arrived and threatened to shoot off everyone's privates."

Kellen grinned. "Julie had a gun?"

"She said she could nail a river rat at fifty paces."

"There's no doubt in my mind," Kellen said. "I ran a check on the house on Commonwealth. It's owned by a holding company. And I was able to trace the holding company back to Ronald Bergman."

"Big surprise."

"Ronald is at the present time raping a forest in Central America and probably doesn't even know he owns the house."

"So you think Kitty and Marty use the house as a stopover for stolen stuff?"

"It's possible."

Kellen didn't like where this was going. Bad enough that Kitty was probably crooked, but now she seemed to be targeting Cate.

"And what about Beast? Hard to believe they want him for his guard dog skills."

"I already looked into Beast. The kennel

owner seems to know Marty. He said Marty was in a couple weeks ago looking for a dog. He took a couple out for a walk and chose Beast. The kennel owner said he gave Marty a break on the price because Beast wasn't show quality and didn't totally have a guard dog personality. I've looked at Beast's collar. It's standard issue from the kennel. No secret pouch filled with stolen diamonds."

"What about his water bowl?"

"I assumed you bought it in some doggie boutique."

"Nope. Marty sent it from Puerto Rico."

"I'll take a look at it when I get home. Did you tell Kitty I have Beast staying with me?"

"No."

"One less thing to worry about," Kellen said, looking at his watch. "I have to get back to the house. How do you feel about all this? Would you feel safer if you moved in with me? Or do you want to stay here?"

"I'll stay here. I'm doing a project for Julie, and I have to leave for work in a couple hours. This is my night to do setup."

Kellen pulled her to him. She was warm in his arms and smelled like cake. He kissed her gently, lingering just long enough to make it painful to pull away. "Wish I had more time," he said. "Call me if you change your mind or need help."

"Give Beast a hug for me."

Chapter
THIRTEEN

A casual observer might look at the slightly paunchy man at the bar and think he was just another customer procrastinating the event of going home. The bar regulars knew the man was the bar owner, Gerald Evian. And Cate knew he only sat in this catatonic stupor when he was panicked. It was fifteen minutes to Marty's first show and Marty was nowhere to be seen. Marty hadn't called. Marty hadn't e-mailed. Marty wasn't answering his phone.

"I'm fucked," Gerald Evian said.

Cate and Gina scurried away from Evian, refilling glasses, making sure no one was thirsty, and adding extra booze to the mixed drinks. In a half hour people would be demanding a drag queen, and they might be more forgiving if they were liquored up.

"Do you think Marty will show?" Gina asked Cate.

"No," Cate said. "I think Marty's in trouble."

Julie had ordered Pugg to escort Cate to work and not let her out of his sight, and Pugg was now sitting at the end of the bar, watching the overhead television. It was close to eleven, and the bar was almost empty. Just a few morose drunks and Pugg and Evian.

"Hey," Pugg said to Cate. "What's the name of the guy you rent from?"

"Marty Longfellow."

"There was just a news flash about him. They fished him out of the Charles River."

All eyes fixed on the television screen, but

the scrolling headline had moved on to game scores.

"Are you sure?" Cate asked.

"It said South End drag queen Marty Longfellow was found washed ashore at the Boston University Bridge. Police were investigating."

Cate felt her stomach go hollow. "Poor Marty."

"I'm out of a job," Gina said.

Evian nodded agreement. "And I'm *truly* fucked."

"We need new entertainment," Gina said.

"Pugg could tell jokes," Pugg said. "Would you like to hear some of Pugg's jokes?"

"No," everyone said in unison.

Kellen strolled into the bar and smiled at Cate. "Closing time?"

"Yes. And we just heard about Marty."

"What did you hear?"

"That they found his body washed ashore at the BU Bridge."

"That's not entirely correct," Kellen said. "I've been listening to the police band. Someone found Marty's wig and a high-heeled pump size fourteen and Marty's evening purse with identification inside at the water's edge. They're dragging the river near the scene, looking for a body."

Cate gave an involuntary shiver at the thought of the police dragging the river for Marty's body. Somehow it was even worse than having Marty's body wash ashore.

"You can leave," Evian said to Cate and Gina. "I'll close up. Give me something to do besides think about bankruptcy."

"Thanks for waiting," Cate said to Pugg when they were outside.

"Pugg had strict instructions not to let you out of Pugg's sight. Pugg shudders to think what would happen to him if he didn't follow instructions. Pugg would be cut off from Julie's affections. Pugg would be left to his own devices for sexual gratification."

Kellen put an arm around Cate. "I'll watch over her for the rest of the night," he said to Pugg.

"No, no, no. Pugg is not allowed to leave Cate's side until Cate is safely locked in her condo. Pugg will follow at a respectful distance."

"It's not necessary to follow at a distance," Kellen said. "But it would be good if you didn't say anything."

"That's too bad," Pugg said, walking fast to keep pace with Kellen's longer legs. "Pugg has many interesting things to say."

"Such as?"

"Pugg is knowledgeable about the gooney bird. The gooney bird is actually an albatross, of the biological family Diomedeidae. They are among the largest of flying birds and range widely in the Southern Ocean and the North Pacific. They have become extinct in the North Atlantic. Pugg does not know why this is."

"I didn't know that," Cate said.

"Gooney birds are highly efficient in the air and can cover great distances with little exertion. They nest on remote oceanic islands and pairs of gooney birds form bonds over several years with the use of ritualistic dances, and that bond will last the life of the pair. Gooney birds are monogamous. Pugg would like to be a gooney bird."

"Wow, that's terrific," Cate said, using her

key fob to unlock the condo building's front door. "I bet you'd make a good gooney bird. Are you going to see Julie now?"

"Yes. Pugg will perform his ritualistic gooney dance and hope Julie is impressed."

They all got into the elevator and Pugg got off at Julie's floor.

Kellen waited for the elevator's doors to close before speaking. "Do you suppose he would actually perform a gooney bird dance?"

Cate laughed out loud. "Yes. And Julie would probably love it."

Kellen followed Cate out of the elevator at the fourth floor and punched her code into the new condo lock. They stepped into the quiet, dark condo and Kellen closed and locked the door behind them.

"Beast is at my house," Kellen said. "And I would feel better if you were there too. I don't like the way the weird factor is escalating on this case."

"I'll throw a few things in an overnight bag," Cate said. "I'm not anxious to stay here. It feels creepy and sad, knowing Marty is at the bottom of the river somewhere."

. . .

Kellen handed Cate a glass of Pinot Grigio and poured a glass for himself.

"You have wineglasses!" Cate said.

"I went shopping today. I thought we needed to celebrate."

"Are we celebrating anything special?"

"Yep. We're celebrating because I got you to take your clothes off last night. And we're celebrating because Julie rescued you this afternoon, and you're safe. And we're celebrating because I was able to remove the bottom on Beast's water bowl and found this. . . ."

Kellen reached into a kitchen drawer and extracted a diamond-and-deep-blue-sapphire necklace.

"That's the most beautiful necklace I've ever seen," Cate said. "Is that the necklace you were looking for?"

"Unfortunately, no."

"What will you do with it?"

"I'll make some inquiries," Kellen said. "And I'll file a report with the police."

Beast softly padded into the kitchen and rubbed against Cate.

"He's all droopy-eyed," Cate said, fondling his ear.

"I'm surprised he even got up. This is *not* a night dog. All day long he has tons of energy. When the sun goes down it's Beast's bedtime, and it takes a forklift to move him."

Cate sipped her wine. "Where do you go from here?"

"I work at getting you out of your clothes again."

Cate grinned. "I meant with your necklace search."

Kellen lounged against the counter. "I need to figure out the Kitty Bergman connection. They were working together. They had a falling out. She came after Marty. And she wanted Beast. Maybe she wanted the necklace in the dog bowl. I have a feeling Marty was holding out on her."

"And what about Marty's agent? What was that about?"

Kellen smiled at Cate. "You're getting into this whole mystery thing, aren't you? You're enjoying some of it."

"It *is* interesting."

"It's a puzzle. You put it together piece by

piece. You just keep working at it until you see the whole picture."

"And this is what you do all day?"

"Pretty much." Kellen put his wineglass on the counter and took Cate into his arms. He kissed the back of her hand, and then the inside of her wrist. "And this is what I intend to do all night. I'm going to start here." He kissed her just below her ear. "And I'm going to keep moving south until we find your favorite spot to get kissed."

Cate was pretty sure she already knew where that spot was, but she thought she'd keep an open mind while he worked his way down.

Cate sprawled in Kellen's king-sized bed and decided it was the most comfortable bed she'd ever slept in. It wasn't too hard. And it wasn't too soft. It was just right. Plus there was plenty of room for three people, although technically speaking one of those people was a dog. Kellen had new pillows and smooth white sheets and a fluffy forest green comforter that was also *just right* for the air-conditioned room. And the best part about the bed, Cate thought, was that it contained Kellen. Not now, but usually. At this precise moment Kellen's side of the bed was empty.

It was Saturday morning and the sun was shining behind honeycomb shades, flooding the room with diffused light. The walls were painted cream and the old-fashioned baseboards and ornate wood doors and crown moldings were dark mahogany. Kellen's bed had a padded dark leather headboard. It was flanked by two marble-topped bedside chests. The only other piece of furniture in the room was an antique mahogany dresser.

Cate checked her watch on the bedside table. Eight o'clock. She'd originally awakened at six, but that led to morning sex, and she'd drifted back to sleep when they were done. And now man and dog were missing.

The door alarm chimed downstairs, and Cate heard footsteps and heavy dog panting coming up the stairs and into the hall. Beast bounded into the bedroom and jumped onto the bed. He turned around a bunch of times and flopped down, his tongue hanging out of his mouth, still panting. Kellen followed Beast into the room.

Cate propped herself up on one elbow. "What did you do to my dog? He's all worn out."

"Your dog is a nutcase. He insists on jumping around like a rabbit. And when I let him loose in the dog park he runs around like a crazy dog. And it's already hot out. It's going to be in the nineties today." Kellen dropped a couple of bags on the bed and set two containers of coffee on the nightstand. "I don't know what you like to eat in the morning so I got one of everything. There's a totally unhealthy breakfast sandwich with egg and sausage and cheese and lots of great grease. There's a carrot cake muffin, a bran muffin, a blueberry muffin. There are a couple bagels with cream cheese. And there are a couple doughnuts. And coffee."

"I'm overwhelmed," Cate said. "I want it all."

Kellen took one of the coffees and opened it. "I've got my name on the honey wheat bagel."

"A healthy breakfast eater?"

"Sometimes." He sat on the edge of the bed and fished his bagel out of the bag. "I've been talking to some of my cop friends and listening to the chatter on the scanner, and they haven't found Marty. Word is that someone in a passing car saw two men pitch a tall woman off the bridge. She was wearing a cocktail dress and heels and carrying a handbag. Marty fits the description. And the witness has seen the wig and shoes and bag found at the water's edge, and while he can't be sure he thinks they belong to the woman he saw."

"Are they still dragging for the body?'

"No. They've stopped."

"That's grim. Could the witness identify the two men if he saw them in a lineup?"

"Don't know. I reminded the police of Pugg's phone call. Needless to say, they weren't happy to learn Kitty Bergman might be involved in something nasty."

Cate chose the maple-glazed doughnut as her first breakfast selection. "We heard about Marty on the eleven o'clock news. When did the witness see him tossed off the bridge?"

"Around three in the morning on Friday.

The shoes and wig and bag were found around eight in the evening."

"Poor Marty."

Kellen sipped his coffee and looked at Cate. "I got the impression you weren't close."

"No. But he was always nice to me."

Kellen broke a chunk off his bagel and fed it to Beast. "It's Saturday. Would you like to do something fun?"

"I'd love to, but I can't. I promised Julie I'd do some typing for her, and I need to get it done before I start school next week."

"I assume that's why you have the large pack of papers and your laptop with you."

"Yeah. Is it okay if I commandeer a corner of your kitchen?"

"You can commandeer whatever you want. If you're going to work, I will too. I have some loose ends I can run down."

When Cate was finished with the doughnut she ate the carrot cake muffin and the breakfast sandwich and drank all her coffee. She gave the blueberry muffin to Beast and dragged herself into the shower.

Chapter
FOURTEEN

Kellen was at his computer when Cate strolled into his office.

"Your mother called while you were in the shower. And your brother. And Sharon the realtor."

Cate called her mother first.

"I knew it was a bad idea to move into that condo," her mother said. "Look at what happens there. First someone falls down the stairs and breaks his neck, and now your roommate is thrown off a bridge. It's all over the news. It's in the papers. And your brother saw it on television. You should be living at home. That building you're in is full of loony people. And where are you? I called your condo and you weren't there. And some man answered your cell phone."

"That was Kellen. Beast and I are staying with him until I get my housing situation straightened out."

"It would straighten out if you came home," her mother said. "I'm sending your father to get you."

"No! Don't do that. I'm fine."

"How could you be fine with people dying all around you? Where are you? Where does this man live? You're not in that same building, are you? That building has bad luck."

Next up was Danny.

"Some guy answered your cell phone," he said. "Should I find him and beat the crap out of him?"

"It was Kellen, and I don't want you beating

the crap out of anyone, especially not Kellen. I like him. I really, really like him, and I won't be happy if you screw it up."

"When did I ever screw anything up for you?"

"How much time do you have?"

"The list isn't *that* long. I don't like this. I think you should go back home with mom and dad. That building has bad juju. And I don't know about this Kellen guy. You hardly know him, and you're living with him."

"I'm staying in his house temporarily until I straighten out my housing situation. It's okay."

"I don't like it. I'm going to come get you. Where are you?"

"*Do not come get me.* I'm fine. And I'm not telling you where I am."

Kellen was watching Cate. "I think I'm in trouble with your family."

"I'm the baby. They're a little overprotective."

"I'm assuming they all want to jump in their car and come get you."

"Yeah. They think I should move back

home. They don't realize it's not an option for me. I love them, but they were driving me crazy when I was at home. They're . . . boisterous. And they fill up a room. Not just my parents, but my grandparents, cousins, aunts, uncles, neighbors. Everyone collects at my parents' house. I couldn't get any work done. I was living at the library. And there were always questions. Where was I? What did I eat for lunch? Who dropped me off? Were they Catholic? And when I had the rare date my father would be waiting up for me!"

"Was it like that for your brothers?"

"My brothers didn't go to college. They went to work and were expected to raise hell. And when they'd raised enough hell the expectation was that they'd get married. And that's exactly what they did."

Kellen pushed back in his chair. "Sounds like my family."

"Did you go to college?"

"No. I was a cop. All the men in my family are cops."

"Did you raise hell?"

"With a vengeance. I did my best to meet

their expectations. And I reached a point where the lifestyle got old, but I never met the woman I was supposed to marry. My sisters are all married and have families. I'm the holdout."

Cate thought she might like to be the woman in Kellen's life. She liked sleeping next to him. And she liked being part of his routine. He was great with Beast, and he'd been great with her nieces. He'd been respectful of her parents but not intimidated. And there was that *thing* . . . the spark of something nameless and intangible that made her warm and happy and sexy when she was near him. The *thing* that had been missing with other men.

"And you stopped being a cop." Cate said.

"It was too rigid, too political. And I felt I was getting a slanted view of human nature, always moving through the dark side of society. I made detective, but it still wasn't satisfying. I felt confined by the structure."

"So you set off on your own?"

"Yes. And I like it. My business is small but profitable. I'm performing a niche service. And I'm good at it."

"You're lucky. You found something you love."

"I did," Kellen said, smiling at her in a way that made her heart stutter.

Don't second-guess him, Cate told herself. It would be exciting to think he was experiencing the same sort of feelings for her that she was having for him, but it was early in the relationship. Don't create a whole falling-in-love fantasy, she thought.

Cate dialed Sharon's number. "One phone call left," she said to Kellen.

"Good grief, I just heard about Marty," Sharon said. "It's all over the news. It's all over the building. This is awful."

"Yeah, I feel really bad," Cate said.

"I didn't know him very well. Just to say hello to."

"He was an okay guy. He kept to himself, but he was always nice to me. And he was . . . interesting."

"I know this is harsh, but it's going to be a black mark on our building. First the agent and now Marty. Condo values are going to drop like a rock, and I have two listings. I need to sell those units. I have a mortgage.

I saw shoes at Saks that I have to have. And what about you? Are you going to try to stay in the condo?"

"No. It feels creepy. And I'll get kicked out anyway. The condo will go into Marty's estate."

"I know about a sweet studio walk-up. It's only a block from here. It would make a great starter property for you."

"I can't buy. I have nothing for a down payment, and I'd have to cut back on classes if I had a mortgage. I could barely afford to rent that room from Marty."

"Beast is going to make it more difficult to find a rental," Sharon said. "Where are you? I went upstairs to your condo, but no one was home. Since a man answered your cell I'm assuming you're either with your parents or Mr. Yummy."

"Mr. Yummy."

"Lucky you. I have a good feeling about him." Sharon sighed into the phone. "I have a good feeling about 2B, but I can't connect."

"Are you sure a man lives there?"

"This morning there was a name under his

door buzzer. Mr. M. How mysterious is that? Mr. M."

"That's pretty mysterious," Cate said. "Did you check around to see if anyone saw Mr. M. fiddling with his name plate?"

"No one saw. He must have done it in the wee hours of the morning. Gosh, I can't imagine what the building will be like without you. Why don't you move in with me? I have an extra bedroom. It would be fun."

"That's really nice of you, but I might have some other options."

"Well, the offer is always there. I have to go. I'm showing a townhouse this morning."

Cate didn't have other options. She had a big dog and no money. What she had were two very good friends, and she didn't want to lose one of those friends by encroaching on her space.

"What are you going to do?" Kellen asked.

Cate shrugged. "I'll find something."

"We might be able to work something out here . . . in exchange for services."

"What sort of services were you thinking about?"

"Cooking. Cleaning. Sex."

"That could get pricey," Cate said. "My cooking doesn't come cheap."

And it could be painful, Cate thought. She would have a hard time tearing herself away from Kellen and his house if it didn't work out. And she still couldn't tell if this was casual sex or something more for Kellen. It was too soon for the "L" word to get spoken out loud. And how do you figure this stuff out?

Her relationship with Beast was much easier. She could promise undying love to Beast, and he'd happily stay around as long as she fed him.

Midmorning Cate's cell phone rang.

"Hey, girlfriend," Julie said. "Where the heck are you? I sent Pugg up to fetch you, but he said nobody's home."

"Pugg is there? Doesn't he sell tires on Saturdays?"

"He has the day off, and I have him runnin' errands. He's such a good soul. So where are you? Are you out with the dawg?"

"I'm at Kellen's house."

"Mr. Yummy? Omigod. I was thinkin' you

might be with him. I want a full report. He's great, right? I can always tell."

"Did you hear about Marty?"

"Hard not to hear about Marty. It's all anyone's talkin' about. It's just so sad. And I hate the thought that you might leave the building. You and Sharon are like sisters to me."

"I like the South End. I'm going to try to get something in the neighborhood."

"Shoot. You could stay here with me. I could even get an extra chaise longue. Only problem is my landlord won't let Beast stay here. Not that there's that much difference between Beast and Patrick Pugg. They both got about the same amount of fur."

"I've got a good start on your pages. I thought I'd stop around after lunch and drop some of them off, so you can see if they're okay."

"Sure. I was hoping you'd do me a favor today, if you have the time. We got the seniors on the party trolley again, and they're asking for more of your cake. My boss said he could use four cakes, and he'd pay for them. And one of them has to be the yellow cake with the white frosting and multicolored sprinkles.

And another wants to be the chocolate chip cake with the creamy chocolate icing."

"He'll pay?"

"Yep."

"It's a deal."

Cate punched the code into the condo lock and pushed the door open. She had Julie's pages tucked under her arm, her purse hung on her shoulder, and a grocery bag balanced on her hip. The condo was silent and felt benign. As far as Cate could tell there was no bad juju lurking behind the drapes or under the bed. She kicked the door closed and went to the kitchen. She'd bought butter, eggs, powdered sugar, and cake mixes. She had the rest of the ingredients already in the condo.

Marty's kitchen still felt empty to Cate. It would have felt better if Beast had been there. And while Cate had mixed feelings about Marty now, she wished he was in the kitchen too. He might not be the guy she thought he was, but she didn't wish him dead.

She went to work buttering and flouring

cake pans, and setting out oil, bowls, the colored sprinkles, and chocolate chips. It would be fun to do this in Kellen's kitchen, she thought. All that space to work. And his kitchen felt like a real house kitchen. It had a big cook's stove, and the beautiful mahogany moldings were everywhere. And the best part about Kellen's kitchen was Kellen. He didn't have a lot of pots and pans. He didn't have a mixer or spatulas or even a toaster, but his presence was felt. His keys were on the counter. A pad and pen. The take-out menu for California Pizza Kitchen and P.F. Chang's left lying out, next to the phone. The knowledge that he was somewhere in the house and could walk through the kitchen at any moment.

Cate closed her eyes and thunked her forehead against an over-the-counter cabinet. She was in bad shape. She was doomed. There was no denying it, she was in love.

Two hours later, Cate had four cakes cooling on racks on the granite countertops, and she had the butter softening for the icing. Plenty of time, she thought. She didn't have to be at work until six. It was three o'clock now. And it wasn't like she had to go back to Kellen's house to get dressed. She still had clothes in the condo.

She was about to add powdered sugar to the butter when the doorbell chimed. She wiped her hands on her jeans and went to the door. She looked out through the peephole and didn't see anyone at first. She looked lower and realized it was Pugg at the door.

"Julie sent Pugg to help," he said to Cate.

"Thanks, but I don't actually need help."

"Pugg would score points if you let him help. Or maybe Pugg could just stand to one side and watch. Pugg would be very quiet."

"Sure. Come on in."

Pugg followed Cate into the kitchen and flattened himself against a wall.

"You won't even know Pugg is here," he said. He craned his neck to see what Cate was doing. "Did you know that some people believe the first cake mix in a box dates back to 1929 with Duncan Hines? Pugg has read that these mixes were lumpy, but he doesn't know from personal experience. Jiffy and Bisquick were introduced in 1930. And General Mills and Pillsbury did not produce cake mix until 1949."

"I didn't know that," Cate said.

"Where is Cate's dog?"

"He's with Kellen. I thought he'd be safer there. Kitty Bergman wanted to take him away."

"Why would Kitty Bergman want Beast?"

"I'm not sure, but I think he might be mixed up in stolen property."

"Pugg is interested in this. If Pugg was a master thief he would implant a microchip under a dog's hide and have Pugg's secret bank accounts recorded on it."

Cate stopped stirring. "Can you do that?"

"Yes. It's common practice to implant microchips in animals for identification purposes. Microchips are tiny transponders approximately the size of a grain of uncooked rice. They carry unique identification numbers and are implanted just below the hide using a needle. They can be easily read with a handheld scanner."

"Can anyone do this?"

"Most often this is done by a veterinarian or breeder, but it would seem to be a simple procedure, that could be done by anyone able to stick a needle in his dog."

"How do you know all this miscellaneous information?"

"Pugg has large blocks of free time while he waits to score with chicks, so he reads books, many of which are filled with interesting but basically useless information."

"What would a scanner look like?"

"Pugg has never seen one, but he imagines it might look like a small television remote."

"Look around the condo while I make icing and see if you can find one. Look in Marty's room first."

Cate was finishing the last cake, piping on small yellow flowers, when Pugg came into the kitchen with the scanner.

"Pugg thinks he found the scanner," he said. "It was in Marty's office and could easily be overlooked in a drawer with other electronic gizmos. Pugg thinks this is the scanner because Pugg could not get it to work the television or DVD player."

Cate took the scanner in her hand. "It's light."

"Yes. The average chip scanner weighs four

ounces and can read transponders operating at 125 and 128 kHz. Pugg believes this particular scanner is Swiss-made to read a fifteen-digit code and needs a transponder operating at 134 kHz. It sells for $179.95 on the Internet and weighs less than three ounces."

"You must have a photographic memory."

"At the risk of ruining your inflated opinion of Pugg, Pugg read most of that on the back of the scanner."

Cate dropped the scanner in her purse and carefully boxed the cakes.

"I got these boxes from the bakery on the corner so everything would stay nice," she said to Pugg. "You take two of them, and I'll take two of them. Just be very careful not to tip them. I don't want the icing to get smushed."

They maneuvered out of the condo with the cakes, and Cate made sure the door was locked behind her. They rode one floor down in the elevator, and carried the cakes into Julie's apartment and set them on her kitchen counter.

"The little old folks are gonna love these cakes," Julie said. "The trolley's coming by special to pick them up."

"Pugg . . . I mean, *I* was very helpful," Pugg said. "I found the scanner for Cate."

"What the dickens is a scanner?" Julie asked.

"It's a device for reading a microchip," Cate said. "We think Marty might have installed one in Beast. It would be a safe way to transport bank codes or safe combinations."

"That sounds real high tech. My cousin Orville used to do something like that. He was a professional balloon swallower. If you wanted something transported somewhere and you didn't want anyone to know, Orville would put it in a balloon and swallow it. It worked real good except the downside was you had to wait a day or two for Orville to poop it out."

"Your cousin Orville was a mule?" Pugg asked. "That's a very dangerous profession."

"Yeah, but if Orville didn't do that he was pretty much unemployable. He once dropped his teeth in the deep fryer at Burger King. He said he sneezed and next thing his dentures were in with the French fries. Lucky for him he was good at carryin' drugs or else he wouldn't have been able to keep up the pay-ments on his double-wide."

"Is Orville still employed in this manner?" Pugg asked.

"No, poor ol' Orville was carryin' a bal-loon from Mexico to Birmingham one day, and it got a little pinhole in it and leaked some of the stuff out into Orville. By the time he got to Birmingham he was foamin' at the mouth. He didn't die, but he's still droolin' and foamin', and he thinks everyone's Walter Cronkite. So my Aunt Madelyn had to put Orville in the Shady Rest Nursing Home. It was a shame, but Orville had a real good run before the pinhole."

"Shit happens," Pugg said. "Excuse my French."

Cate put Julie's typed pages on the counter next to the cakes. "I have about twenty pages here," Cate said. "Take a look at them and make sure they're okay. I have to run. I want to talk to Kellen before I leave for work."

"Do you need Pugg to escort you?" Julie asked.

"No. I'll be fine."

"Maybe you could stop in and say hello to Sharon for a second," Julie said. "She's nutty over 2B again, and I haven't been able to do anything with her. I swear she's such a sensible, grounded person, except for her shoes and 2B."

Chapter
FIFTEEN

Cate left Julie's apartment and rang Sharon's bell. No answer. On a hunch Cate went down a level and found Sharon in the hall, looking wild-eyed and wringing her hands.

"What's up?" Cate said. "You look a little unhinged."

"The door's open."

"Excuse me?"

"The door to 2B. Take a closer look. It's open just a smidgeon."

Cate took a closer look. "Yep," she said. "It's open."

"Someone's in there," Sharon said.

"It could be the housekeeper. Or the plumber again."

"It's him," Sharon said. "Mr. M. He's home. I can feel it. My skin is tingling."

"Oh boy."

"What should I do?"

"Nothing?"

"Should I ring the bell and tell him his door is open?"

"Yeah. Ring the bell."

"I can't. I'm too nervous."

Cate rang the bell.

"Omigod," Sharon said, her hand in a death grip on Cate's arm. "I can't believe you did that."

"When he answers just tell him his door was open."

A couple of moments passed and no one answered the door. Cate rang the bell again. No response.

"Maybe he's dead on the floor," Sharon said. "Maybe this is the death building."

"Maybe you're a fruitcake."

"Do you think we should go in and investigate?"

"No."

"Okay then," Sharon said, pushing the door a little more open, peeking inside. "But it was your idea."

"It wasn't my idea. I said no!"

"Hello-o-o," Sharon called softly. "Anybody home?"

"That's it. I'm leaving," Cate said.

Sharon had hold of Cate's shirt. "You can't abandon me. We're in this together."

"You're insane! You're in this all by yourself. Let go of my shirt."

"Please. Please. Please. I have to find out about this guy. And suppose he really is dead or hurt or something. It's our obligation as neighbors to help him, right?"

"If he's dead it won't matter. And if he's hurt he should be moaning. Do you hear moaning?"

They both stopped and listened.

"No moaning," Sharon said.

"He probably took trash to the trash room."

"He'd be back by now if he was on a trash run." Sharon had inched her way into the living room. "This is nice. Very calm without being sterile. Earth tones. Flat-screen television. African fertility statue. Framed movie posters on his wall. Fun but not expensive. Excellent Tibetan area rug."

"I think we should leave," Cate said.

"Not until I see his bedroom."

"Okay, but make it fast. I feel uncomfortable."

Sharon tiptoed in her heels into the bedroom.

"Why are you tiptoeing?" Cate asked.

"I don't know. I can't help myself. It's what you do when you're being sneaky." She stopped and looked around the room. "King-sized bed. Completely rumpled. He's a thrasher. Other than that, the room is neat. Crossword puzzle book on his nightstand. I think I could live with him."

"You don't even know him! He could be Jack the Ripper."

"Jack the Ripper is dead," Sharon said.

"Okay, he could be Frank the Ripper."

Cate looked at her watch. She'd been in the condo for not quite five minutes, but it seemed like five hours.

"I haven't seen any photos of kids or wives or girlfriends," Sharon said.

"Also no photos of Mr. M."

They were in the master bedroom and two rooms away Cate and Sharon heard the front door click closed and the bolt get thrown.

Cate felt all the air leave her lungs. Mr. M. was home. It was a nightmare come true. *Run!* Cate's brain was screaming. *Run!* Cate looked around. Nowhere to run. The window, she thought. Go out the window. Okay, so they were two flights up. Probably she'd just break both legs. She could deal. Mental head slap. That was dumb. The window was no good. They had to hide. The bathroom? The closet? Cate was in a panic attack. Sweating. Can't breathe. Heart racing. Brain running down dead-end streets.

"The bed!" Sharon said. "Get under the bed."

It was a faux antique mahogany four-poster. No dust ruffle but the quilt was over-sized and hung low. Sharon dropped to the floor and belly crawled, barely fitting under the box spring. Cate followed her, and they lay side by side, eyes wide.

There were muffled footsteps on the rug and shoes came into view. Nike running shoes. Maybe size eleven. Jeans breaking on the shoes. Cate couldn't see more. The shoes were walking around, doing things. Something was placed on the bedside table. A dresser drawer was opened and closed. The shoes were back by the bed. A brown-and-orange T-shirt was dropped onto the floor. The shoes were kicked off. White athletic socks were peeled off the feet. The jeans hit the floor and navy briefs followed.

Cate and Sharon stared out at the pile of clothes and the naked feet and didn't breathe.

This is a train wreck, Cate thought. What on earth would she say if she got caught? *Sharon is in love with you even though she's never seen you and has no idea who you are, and so we sneaked into your apartment and looked around and hid under the bed.* Yeah, that would fly. Not.

The feet walked into the bathroom, there was the sound of the shower being turned on, and then there was the sound of the shower curtain being drawn.

Cate and Sharon locked eyes and backed out from under the bed. They quietly tiptoed out of the bedroom and sprinted through the rest of the condo, out the door, down the hall, and up a flight of stairs. They threw themselves into Sharon's condo and locked the door.

"I'm having a heart attack," Sharon said. "What are the symptoms? Are they profuse sweating and burning in the chest?"

"No. I think that's a hot flash."

"I'm too young for a hot flash," Sharon said. "Aren't I?"

"I don't know. I guess some women go into menopause earlier than others. How old are you?"

Sharon looked around, making sure no one else was in her apartment. "I'm pushing forty."

"No! You look *much* younger."

"Forty! And I just had a hot flash. Next thing I'll be finding *Modern Maturity* in my mailbox. And my breasts will get saggy. And I'll have to start popping antacids. And I'll have to start getting Botox shots. Well, okay, so I already get a little Botox, but it's more preventative, right? And all I have in my life is some phantom man. I haven't gotten laid in over a year!" Sharon wailed.

"You get Botox?"

"Just a tiny shot between the eyebrows so I don't look grumpy. No one wants to buy a house from a grumpy realtor. So what did you think of him?" Sharon asked.

"Who?"

"Mr. M. I thought he had nice feet. And the navy Calvins could be sexy."

"You need to get out more," Cate said. "Have you thought about a dating service?"

"Tried that. I always got stuck with the check."

Chapter
SIXTEEN

Cate bolted out of the condo building and hit the ground running. She wanted to show Kellen the scanner, and she needed to shower and change her clothes. It was close to five o'clock and the traffic was heavy. The temperature was in the high eighties, but a stiff breeze ripped down the street. A storm was blowing in. She reached the townhouse and realized she didn't have a key. She rang the bell and prayed Kellen was home. She hadn't thought to call first.

Kellen opened the door, and Cate rushed past him.

"I'm late," Cate said.

Kellen snagged her arm, and pulled her to him and kissed her. "What time do you need to be at work?"

"Six. But I have to take a shower and get dressed."

Kellen nuzzled her neck. "You smell good. You smell like birthday cake. You always smell like cake."

"I made four cakes for the party trolley, and Julie said her boss would pay me for them."

"I'd pay to nibble on *you*," Kellen said.

"Really? Do you . . . um, pay for sex?"

He smiled down at her. "No. But you'd be worth it."

"I guess that's a compliment."

"It's conversation. My plan is to keep talking to you so you stay pressed up against me."

Kellen hardly needed a plan. He was warm and hard . . . some places harder than others. Cate was quickly losing her sense of priority.

"It's a good plan, but I've got to take a shower. And I have something to show you." Cate scrounged around in her purse and pulled out the scanner.

"What is it?"

"It's a scanner. It reads microchips that get implanted in pets for identification purposes. It was in Marty's condo."

Beast's toenails could be heard scrabbling on the wood floor as he turned a corner and galloped toward Cate. He put the brakes on too late and plowed into her, buckling her knees.

Cate bent to hug Beast. "I missed you," she said to Beast. "Did you have a good afternoon?"

"We went for a walk, and he played with his friends in the dog park," Kellen said. "He drank a bowl of water and slobbered it all over the kitchen floor. And then he took a nap. If I can convince you and Beast to stay here, I'm going to have my cleaning lady come more than once a week. I might even buy a mop."

"Wow, buying a mop is pretty drastic for a bachelor like you."

"It's a small price," Kellen said.

He looked at the scanner and pushed the button to turn it on. "I should have thought of this. I know microchip use is common. It just didn't pop up on my radar screen." He passed the scanner over the scruff of Beast's neck, and numbers appeared on the readout.

"Here's the problem," Kellen said. "We don't know what these numbers mean. This could just be an ID chip. We know Kitty Bergman wanted Beast, but maybe she wanted the water bowl."

"Maybe I should ask her," Cate said.

Kellen grinned. "You're going to call her up and ask her?"

"Yeah."

"I like it. Do you have her phone number?"

"No. Get her phone number, and I'll jump in the shower, and I'll call when I get out."

"Do you need help in the shower?"

"No! I'm late."

"You're not late yet," Kellen said.

"I will be if you help in the shower."

Kellen and Beast were waiting in the bedroom when Cate stepped out of the bathroom.

"I got the number," Kellen said. "Are you sure you want to do this?"

Truth was, she'd rather cut off her thumb than call Kitty Bergman. Unfortunately, Cate didn't think Kitty was going to give up on Beast. Kitty was a woman who was used to getting what she wanted. If the necklace in the water bowl was the prize, and Beast was simply incidental, then Cate could keep Beast safe by telling Kitty the necklace had been found and turned over to the police. And that's why Cate was going to call scary Kitty Bergman.

"Yeah," Cate said. "Dial her up."

Kellen punched the number in and handed Cate the headset.

"Hey, how's it going?" Cate said to Kitty.

"Who is this?"

"Cate Madigan. Beast's mom. I was wondering if you still wanted Beast now that Marty's . . . gone."

"Of course. Marty would want me to take care of his dog."

"The thing is, Beast is used to me. We've

sort of bonded. So I thought it might be best for me to adopt him."

"That's very sweet of you, but out of the question."

"And by the way, the strangest thing happened. His water bowl fell apart and there was a diamond-and-sapphire necklace in it. Can you imagine? Anyway, I gave it over to the police, of course."

"Of course," Kitty said.

"Do you still want Beast?"

"It's really what Marty would want. Marty would want me to have his dog. And if you don't give him to me I'll track you down, and when I'm done with you, you will be dust."

"Okay then. Good conversation," Cate said. And she hung up.

Kellen was watching Cate. "Well?"

"She wants Beast."

"Your face turned white at the end there."

"She said she was going to make me into dust."

"That's extreme."

Cate checked her watch. "Shoot! I have to go."

"I'll walk with you," Kellen said, putting the headset in its cradle. "I don't want the Wicked Witch turning you into dust."

Gina and Cate stood side by side looking across the bar at the half-empty room.

"Evian's going to have to find a Marty substitute real quick," Gina said. "This place is going to tank."

"Yeah, it's amazing how fast everyone jumped ship," Cate said.

Gina focused on Evian sitting at the end of the bar, head down, fingering a bowl of bar nuts, presumably looking for something special. A cashew maybe. "Poor guy," Gina said. "He looks real depressed. I guess he's got real problems."

Cate had a suspicion Evian's problems were pale compared to her problems. Evian might lose the bar, but Kitty Bergman was going to turn Cate into dust. The one bright note was that Cate felt confident Kellen would take care of Beast.

Marty's keyboard guy and bass player were on stage, banging out some songs without

Marty. A few people paid attention. Most kept their noses in their drinks. Pugg was on duty, sitting at a high-top table, watching Cate as if she might at any moment vanish in a poof of smoke.

Cate motioned to Pugg to come to the bar.

"Pugg is at your service," he said, climbing onto a stool.

"I know you have instructions to keep your eye on me, but I'm really okay. It's nice of you to stay here, but Kellen will be picking me up, and nothing's going to happen in the bar."

"Be that as it may, Pugg has promised Julie he would not let you out of his sight. And if Pugg does not fulfill that promise, Pugg won't get any tonight."

Cate smiled. He was endearing in a very bizarre way. "Do you like Julie?"

"Julie is a saint. Pugg doesn't deserve Julie, but he'll bang her all the same."

"Is that all you're interested in? Sex?"

"Defense mechanism," Pugg said. "The truth is I'm nuts about her, and it scares the bejeezus out of me. How could anyone like that love anyone like me?"

"I have a feeling under all that Pugg stuff you're really a good guy."

"I don't even know what's under the Pugg stuff anymore."

"You should take some time to find out," Cate said.

The bar phone rang at ten o'clock and Gina passed it over to Cate.

"It's for you," Gina said. "Didn't give a name."

Cate drew another draft for a customer and took the phone.

"Cate?"

"Yes?"

"Don't faint or anything, but it's Marty."

"That's impossible. Marty's . . . you know."

"I swam to shore. I just lost my wig and a shoe and my purse. That was one of my favorite wigs too. I paid three hundred bucks for that wig. Here, listen to this." And he sang a couple bars from "Over the Rainbow."

"Omigod," Cate said. "You sound just like Marty."

"I am Marty! And I'm locked out of my condo. What the hell is that thing on the door?"

"People were breaking in, so I changed the lock to something that couldn't be picked."

"No shit. Houdini couldn't crack that lock."

"Where are you?"

"I'm in the alley behind the bar. I've been living in a packing crate about a block from Evian's, trying to be invisible. Being dead has some advantages, it turns out. Mostly that no one wants to kill you again."

"Maybe you should go to the police."

"Not an option. I need to get into the condo. If I can get into the condo I can leave the country. And I need to see my dog. He's in the condo, right?"

"Actually, he's staying with a friend of mine."

"How could you do that? I asked *you* to take care of him. Is he close? Does he have the beautiful bowl I sent him?"

Cate turned her back to the room and lowered her voice. "Marty, I found the necklace in the bowl."

There was a beat of silence and then a sigh. "Fuck," Marty said.

"I turned it over to the police."

"Did you tell them where it came from?"

"No."

"Cate, you have to help me. I need to get away from Kitty Bergman. The woman is insane. The only way I can get away is to get into the condo. And I need the dog. You need to go get him and bring him to the condo. And please do it now. Tell Evian you got the curse or something. I can't keep living in this packing crate. I need some decent food. I need a safe place to sleep. I need a manicure."

"Out of morbid curiosity, how are you making this call?"

"I stole a cell phone. It's nice. It's one of those new Motorolas. Unfortunately it's pink and not at all my color palate."

"Okay, I'll meet you at the condo. And I'll have my friend bring Beast."

"I swear I'll make this up to you. I really appreciate this."

Cate hung up and dialed Kellen.

"I just got a call from Marty. I know it was him because he sang 'Over the Rainbow' to me. He wants to get into the condo. I told him I'd have you bring Beast over, and I'd let him in."

"I don't want you going to the condo alone. I'll pick you up at Evian's."

There were a handful of customers at high-topped bar tables and half the stools were filled at the bar. One hour until closing. No need to stay open late without Marty Longfellow on stage. Gina could easily handle the orders, Cate thought.

Cate made sure her tabs were in order. She told Gina and Evian she wasn't feeling well and was leaving early. She got her purse from the back room and quietly walked through the dim bar.

"I'm leaving early," she told Pugg. "Kellen is picking me up. Thanks for watching over me."

Pugg nodded.

Cate walked out the front door and stood under the glow of the overhead globe light. A thunderstorm had just passed through, and the sidewalks were glistening wet and steaming themselves dry. There were few people on the street, most having been chased indoors by the storm.

A black town car pulled to the curb in front of Evian's, the passenger-side door opened, and a man got out. It took Cate a moment to place him. He was one of Kitty Bergman's goons. Cate turned to the bar and had her hand on the door when she was yanked back. There were a flash and a sizzle and then it was all black for a moment. Weak legs, scrambled brain. She stumbled and was pulled up. Hands under her armpits. Someone dragging her. And then she was in the car, in the backseat, next to a strange man. Her hands were shackled. She wasn't sure how that happened. She gave her head a small shake to focus and looked hard at the man next to her. It was Marty. He was bearded and unkempt, in baggy, dirty jeans and a wrinkled denim shirt.

"You set me up," Cate said to Marty.

"No," Marty said. They were out here waiting for you, and they saw me walk out of the alley."

One of the men in the front seat turned to

Cate. "Yeah, we were real lucky. At first we didn't recognize him. We thought he was dead. He caught our attention because he didn't shuffle along like a guy on the street. And then we realized it was Marty."

"Why were you waiting for me?"

"I'm sorry," Marty said. "When they captured me the first time I told them about the water bowl and the microchip in the dog. And unfortunately, you have the dog."

"Yeah," the guy in the front said. "Marty avoids pain." He had his cell phone in his hand and he punched in a number. "We have her," he said to someone on the other end. "And we got someone else too. You're gonna love this. We got Marty. Turns out he can swim."

They were on Columbus and turned onto Dartmouth. Traffic was slow. Saturday night and it had rained. Everyone was in a car. Cate turned and looked out the back window, and saw Pugg running behind the town car. She was at once grateful and horrified. She didn't want them to capture Pugg too. She was afraid Pugg wouldn't avoid pain.

She was afraid Pugg had too much hero in him for his own good.

"What happened to me back there?" Cate asked.

"Stun gun," the guy in the front said. "We just gave you a jolt. We gave Marty enough to curl his hair when we threw him off the bridge." He looked at Marty. "Who would have thought you'd swim out of it?"

Cate had a sick feeling in her stomach, and her heart was thudding in her chest. The atmosphere in the car was more conversational than confrontational, but her hands were cuffed in front of her, and she was being abducted. Marty had apparently told them what they needed to know, and they'd thrown him off a bridge, all the same. She'd be happy to get Beast and let them wand the number off him as long as he was returned to her unhurt. Even if Marty was a thief it was hard to believe he had anything valuable enough to go to all this trouble and risk exposure.

The town car turned left onto Commonwealth and Cate caught sight of Pugg running, shirttails flapping, on the sidewalk beside them. He had his eyes on the car and ran flat out into a woman walking a sheepdog. The last Cate saw of Pugg he was sprawled on the ground and he wasn't moving.

The town car cut around to the alley behind the house with the red door and pulled into a parking space.

"We're going to get out now, and we're going to walk to the back door and go in," the guy in the front said to Cate. "If you make a sound, I'll hit you with the stun gun. If you struggle, I'll hit you with the stun gun. If you try to run, I'll knock you down, and then I'll hit you with the stun gun."

"Okey dokey," Cate said. "Got it."

Cate and Marty were walked through the back door into the kitchen, into the center hall, and up a flight of stairs to a bedroom.

"We're gonna leave you here, and don't try to do anything cute like jump out a window. We'd hear you screaming in pain when you hit the ground, and we'd drag your broken bones back in here and lock you in this room again."

The two men left the room, locking the door behind them.

"I imagine we're waiting for Kitty to arrive," Marty said. "Ick. She's like the slime monster dressed in Chanel. It just isn't *right*."

"What's the deal with Kitty Bergman and you? I know you steal jewelry. What's Kitty got to do with it?"

Chapter
SEVENTEEN

Marty sat on the edge of the bed. "I might as well tell you. The bitch will probably kill me anyway. It's really a pretty sweet deal. Or at least it was until Kitty went gonzo. Kitty and I have been friends forever. I knew her before she married Ronald Bergman. I knew her when she was a waitress at the Domino Diner on the North Shore. And Kitty knew I was always good with my hands. Not that I ever stole anything of worth. It was just a hobby. A way to amuse myself.

"Anyway, several years ago, Kitty approached me about using my unique skill for good purpose. Kitty was involved in every charity known to mankind, and Ronald was a big tightwad. Kitty would squeeze money out of him by padding furniture bills and whatnot, and then she'd use it for her charities, but it wasn't enough. Kitty made promises she couldn't keep. So she came up with this plan where she'd recommend me as entertainment for a function, and then when I had a free moment I'd look around for a nice piece of jewelry. When I got back to Boston I'd fence the jewelry and give the money to Kitty, and she'd give me a commission.

"It was really quite noble, I thought. I was taking a bauble from the rich, and Kitty was giving the proceeds to the poor. You might say I was Robin Hood."

Cate wondered if Robin Hood had a cave full of original art and a Mercedes hidden away in Sherwood Forest.

"Well, we did this for a couple years, and

I started to get worried. Kitty was out of control, needing more and more money, and I felt like we were taking too much. I was fencing the pieces in Europe as added security, but even so, it was becoming excessive. So I had a plan. I decided I would squirrel some of the jewelry away until it wasn't so hot. And when I had enough jewelry set aside I'd quit for a while. Then we could fence the pieces as we needed money."

"And Kitty didn't like this," Cate said.

"Kitty signed on for massive amounts of money to the hospital and to the literacy program. All wonderful causes, but it meant I'd be working nonstop for the next forty years. I told her she had to find a different way to fund her charities. And then I made the mistake of telling her about the retirement cache. She insisted I cash it in immediately, and I refused. Most of the pieces in the vault were one of a kind and still too hot to take to market. It would have been suicide to float all that jewelry."

"So she threw you off a bridge?"

"I knew she'd be pissed. I didn't think she'd be *that* pissed. I mean, I told her everything she wanted to know. I told her about Beast and the safe. There really was no reason to throw me off the bridge. Personally, I think it's her age. You know, hormonal. My new rule is never engage in business with a menopausal woman."

"What about your agent? Was he menopausal?"

Marty put his hand to his heart. "That dreadful man! It wasn't enough he was sucking my blood getting twenty percent of everything I made. He tried to blackmail me. I was careless after a gig last month and Irwin saw a necklace in my suitcase. I wasn't expecting him to stop by, and he just popped in while I was unpacking. It used to be that I'd go straight to Kitty's house on Commonwealth and use the safe until I was ready to sell the piece. When I decided I needed to start setting some aside, I had a safe installed in my condo and that's how Irwin saw the necklace. I got in late, and I had my suitcase open. I told him it was part of my Judy Garland collection, but he didn't buy it. He'd seen a news clip about the robbery and they'd broadcast a picture of the necklace."

"So you pushed him down the stairs?"

"No! Good heavens. I'm a thief, not a murderer. I just got so enraged. I mean, it was so unjust that Irwin would want to extort money from me. And I paid him once and then he came back again. Can you imagine? The man was just so disreputable. Well, after all, what can you expect? He's an agent, which is just another word for parasite if you ask me."

Cate thought Marty probably had a different opinion of agents when he was out of work and couldn't get a job on his own, but heck, what did she know about showbiz?

"I noticed a knife was missing from the kitchen," Cate said.

"Actually, it was very satisfying. I went kind of berserk when he asked for more money, and I punched him in the nose. It was the first time I've ever punched anyone, and I was really good at it. I just went *pop*, right on his beak, and he started bleeding and yelling. And then I kind of got into it and grabbed the carving knife and told him I was going to cut him up into little pieces. And that was when he ran out of the condo and tried to get the elevator, but I was right behind him with the knife, so he took the stairs and slipped and fell and broke his neck. Personally, I think it was karma."

Cate looked around the room. It looked like it had been furnished in pieces Kitty no longer wanted in her big house. A queen-sized bed with a cream-colored quilted spread. A tufted headboard in peach tones. An Oriental area rug at the foot of the bed. An ornate mahogany chest of drawers. Audubon prints in slim walnut frames. She'd noticed as they walked through that there were two bedrooms on this floor. She suspected this wasn't the bedroom Marty used when he stayed in the house. There were no personal touches in the room. No photos, no books or magazine, no mints or keys or spare change. And she couldn't see Marty enduring the peach headboard. It was nice, but it very much wasn't Marty.

"I suppose we're waiting for Kitty," Cate said.

"I suppose we are. Saturday night. She probably got called out of some high-society dinner party. She won't be pleased about that." Marty smiled. "That's a little heart-warming."

They could hear the very faint sound of a door opening and closing downstairs. Muffled conversation. Footsteps on the stairs.

The bedroom door opened and one of the men looked in. "She wants to talk to you downstairs."

Cate and Marty filed down the stairs and met Kitty in the center hall. She was dressed in a white Armani suit with black trim, and she had a classic Chanel bag hung on her shoulder.

"This is fun," Kitty said to Marty. "I'll get to throw you off a bridge for a second time. I think this time we'll attach something to your ankle . . . like a Volkswagen."

"Why do you want to throw me off a bridge?" Marty asked. "What's the big deal?"

"I don't trust you."

"If I go to the police, they'll lock me up and throw the key away."

"Yes, but you could go to my husband."

"Oh," Marty said. "I hadn't thought of that."

"Now," Kitty said, turning to Cate. "I

need the dog. How are we going to go about solving this dilemma?"

"I could call and ask my friend to bring the dog to the condo," Cate said. "Or I could go get Beast and bring him myself."

"I like option number one," Kitty said. "Call your friend."

"I don't have my phone," Cate said. "Your man took my purse."

The purse appeared, and Cate rummaged around in it, looking for her phone, her hands still cuffed. She found the phone and punched Kellen's number in, and had the phone to her ear when both the front and back doors crashed open.

Kellen was at the front door, gun drawn, and Julie and Pugg burst through the kitchen. Julie had a gun in her hand, and Pugg was wielding a meat mallet that Cate assumed he had picked up en route. One of Kitty's men pulled a gun, and Kitty ripped it out of his hands and grabbed Cate.

"Freeze," Kitty said. "Everyone back off because I'll kill her, I swear I will. I've worked too hard to let it all slip away from me now. I started out licking envelopes for the hospital silent auction, and now I'm just inches from being elected to the board. The board! Do you have any idea how difficult it is to get elected to the board? Do you know what that means? It means I chair the Twinkle Ball. *I* get to do the seating chart. Kitty Bergman from Quincy gets to do the seating chart for the Twinkle Ball! Two years ago that bitch Patty Fuch did the chart and gave me balcony seating. I was wearing Herrara, and no one saw me. No one saw the Harry Winston necklace. No one saw the Valentino shoes. Now I'm going to be elected to the board, and I'm going to kick that cow to the curb. Patty Fuch will get the table next to the frigging men's room."

"Kitty," Marty said, "can you spell nutsy cuckoo?"

"Shut up, you traitor. You're just a common thief in ladies panties."

"Actually I don't wear ladies panties. I wear briefs that are designed to minimize the male contour."

"As soon as I get my hands on that dog and the jewelry you stole from me, I'm going to minimize your *entire* contour," Kitty said.

Beast had been standing behind Kellen. He gave a low growl, pushed Kellen aside, and lunged at Kitty. He clamped his teeth onto Kitty's purse strap, ripping it off her shoulder and sending the gun flying.

"That's a Chanel bag!" Kitty cried. "For heaven's sake, someone do something. He's slobbering on vintage Chanel."

Beast shook the bag until he was convinced it was dead and then he turned on Kitty. He gave a loud *woof*, put his two front paws on her chest, knocked her over, and sat on her.

"Help," Kitty said.

"What a good ol' dawg," Julie said. "My neighbor Jimmy Spence had a guard dog once, and anyone talked cross-eyed to Jimmy that dog would rip you to shreds and then he'd knock you down and hump on you. It wasn't pretty."

"See, Kitty. Things could be worse. Beast could be a humper," Cate said.

Kellen looked at Cate. "Are you okay?"

"Yep. Are you?"

"No. I'm a mess. I've never been so scared in my life. Pugg called and said you were kidnapped and my heart stopped."

"I would have rescued you myself," Pugg said to Cate, "but I was temporarily unconscious."

"Poor little Pugg," Julie said. "Soon's we get this cleaned up I'm gonna take you home and make you real comfy. You're my hero."

Pugg looked like he would begin purring at any moment.

Kellen got the handcuff key from one of the men and took the cuffs off Cate.

"The numbers from Beast's microchip open a safe in the condo," Cate said to Kellen.

"I searched everywhere," Kellen said. "I didn't see a safe."

"It's there," Marty said. "You just didn't recognize it."

"Is there a closet in this house that can be locked from the outside and not opened from the inside?" Kellen asked Marty.

"There's an owner's closet upstairs."

Kellen checked the two men and Kitty for extra keys and cell phones, cuffed the two men together with Cate's shackles, marched them upstairs with Kitty, and locked the three of them in the closet.

"They'll be okay here for a while, at least

until I decide how to handle this," Kellen said. "Let's go back to the condo and see what we find there."

Everyone trooped out to Kellen's car and stood looking at the Mustang.

"We're not all going to fit," Kellen said.

"You go on ahead," Julie said. "Pugg and I will find our way home."

Chapter
EIGHTEEN

Marty, Kellen, and Beast stepped out of the elevator with Cate, hurried down the hall, and waited while Cate punched in the code to unlock Marty's front door.

"Okay," Kellen said to Marty when they were all inside. "Where is the safe?"

"I don't think I should tell you," Marty said. "I appreciate the rescue, but I'd prefer not to reveal the safe." He gave Kellen his best Doris Day smile. "However, I'd be more than happy to reward you when I feel it's time to move some of the merchandise."

"Here's more bad news," Kellen said to Marty. "I'm a private recovery agent, and you have property belonging to at least one of my clients. You can open the safe now, or you can open the safe when the police get here."

"But I'm Robin Hood," Marty said. "We were using the money for charitable purposes." He flicked his eyes to the Warhol on the wall. "Almost all of it."

"And what about the dead agent?" Kellen asked.

"It was an accident. He was in a panic, and he slipped and fell down the stairs, I swear on my mother's grave."

"Oh, I'm so sorry," Cate said.

"Well, actually she isn't dead," Marty said. "I was swearing pre-mortem."

Kellen didn't show much, and Cate suspected he wasn't buying it. For that matter, she wasn't sure she bought the whole package, but she did feel a tug of compassion for Marty. He looked pathetic in his raggedy clothes. He had a gash on his forehead, and a large bruise and abrasion on his right cheek-bone. His right eye was partially swollen. And he truly did need a manicure.

"Are you going to turn me over to the police?" Marty asked.

"I haven't decided," Kellen said. "I'm not in the fugitive apprehension business, but I have an obligation as a citizen to come forward when I have information about a crime."

"Suppose I open the safe and give you all the jewelry and promise not to ever steal again."

"Evian really does need him at the bar," Cate said. "And even though Kitty's motives weren't great, she still did a lot of good for the community."

Kellen looked at Cate. "Aside from the fact that the agent accident could be pure baloney, if we don't inform the police about Marty we could become accomplices to multiple crimes."

"I just have a hard time thinking about Marty sitting in jail. And it seems a shame that he can't go on entertaining people."

"Okay, here's the deal," Kellen said to

Marty. "I'm going to give you a twenty-four-hour head start. You can leave the country, or you can go to the police yourself and confess. If you go to the police with a decent lawyer, you can probably plea bargain and rat out Kitty Bergman, and get a very reduced sentence."

"I'll take it," Marty said.

"Now show us the safe."

"You're going to love this. It's in the utility room."

Marty led the way, and Kellen and Cate and Beast followed.

"I was worried about Kitty," Marty said. "And I knew she'd hired those two goons who would do anything. And I mean *anything*. So I had this safe installed just in case things got nasty, and the goons got nosey. It opens with a fifteen-digit code, and I have no head for numbers. I can barely remember my phone number. I didn't want to write the code down because I was afraid they'd find the paper. So I had it injected into the dog when I took him for a walk before I bought him. I figured even if someone wanded him they'd just think it was an ID number. What I didn't count on was Kitty's ability to inflict pain and my inability to tolerate it. The first time they hit me I blurted it all out."

The utility room was nothing more than a closet off the hall. It contained a water heater, a furnace, and two fuse boxes. No safe that Cate could see.

"Have you ever had to flip a circuit breaker?" Marty asked Cate.

"No."

Marty opened the doors to the two fuse boxes. Both looked identical. The circuit breakers on the top box were labeled. Bath, kitchen, bedrooms, and living areas. The circuit breakers on the bottom box weren't labeled. Marty flipped one of the switches quickly three times and the panel popped open to reveal a wall safe behind it.

"Nice," Kellen said. "I'd actually wondered about the second fuse box."

Kellen punched in the chip code and the safe clicked open.

"I've saved all my favorite pieces," Marty said on a sigh, taking a blue velvet box from the safe. Truth is, some of these I'm not sure I ever could have voluntarily parted with."

Kellen opened the box and unwrapped the jewelry. Four necklaces, two bracelets, a broach, two rings, and two pairs of earrings, all in their own blue velvet wraps.

"The necklace I've been looking for is here," Kellen said. "And there are four more pieces that are on my list. If you decide to turn yourself in to the police, I'll corroborate your story and testify against Kitty Bergman, but you have to agree to give Beast to Cate."

"Of course Cate can have Beast if she wants him. And she's welcome to stay in my condo for as long as she wants if I'm . . . sent away. I'll go to the police first thing in the morning," Marty said. "And in the meantime I'm going to lock my front door and not let anyone in . . . just in case Kitty has escaped from the closet."

Cate and Kellen and Beast took the elevator to the lobby.

"What should we do about Kitty?" Cate asked. "We can't just leave her in the closet all night."

"I'm sure she's out of the closet by now. She was locked in there with two big guys, and the door wasn't that strong."

Julie, Pugg and Sharon were in the lobby.

"We ran into Sharon coming home from the movies," Julie said. "And we're all here waiting to see what happened."

"Everything's fine," Cate said. "Kellen found the necklace he's been looking for, and Marty is upstairs, safe in his condo. He has some things to sort through and some decisions to make."

Sharon gave her head a small shake. "You never know about people. Who would have thought Marty and Kitty would be in business together, stealing jewelry?"

"It's like he's the Pink Panther," Julie said. "I loved those movies. I think my next book will be about Marty."

A man pushed through the front door into the lobby and went to the bank of mailboxes. He took a key out of his pocket and opened the box labeled Mr. M.

All eyes were glued to the man.

"Omigosh, are you Mr. M.?" Julie asked.

"Yes. Michael Menzenbergenfelt. My name wouldn't fit in the space."

He was in his midforties. Dark hair, receding hairline, average build gone a little soft around the middle, average height, pleasant smile. And Cate knew he had nice ankles and was slightly flatfooted.

"We've been wonderin' about you," Julie said. "You're the man of mystery around here. No one ever sees you."

"I'm a writer. Historical fiction. Mostly set around Bonaparte. Between trying to make a deadline and traveling on book tour I've been keeping odd hours. I haven't really been here that much."

"Julie's a writer, too," Cate said.

"Are you published?" Michael asked.

"No. But maybe someday. I'm just starting out."

"Her book is wonderful," Cate said.

"Let me know if I can help," Michael said. "I assume we're neighbors."

"Yep, we're 4A, 3A, and 3B," Julie said.

Sharon stepped up. "Sharon Vizzallini in 3B." She gave him her card. "In case you need real estate."

"Sorry," he said, "I don't need real estate." He looked down at her left hand. No ring. "But maybe dinner sometime?"

"Sure," Sharon said. "Tomorrow at six?"

"I've read your books," Kellen said to Mr. M. "I'm a fan. I think the Bonaparte years were fascinating."

Cate and Kellen stood staring at Kellen's bed. Beast was on it, sprawled across the entire width. Beast opened an eye and looked at them, and the eye slid closed.

"You're going to have to move him," Cate said.

"Me? He's *your* dog."

"Yes, but he's big, and he gets cranky when you wake him."

"Are you telling me you're still afraid of your own dog?"

Cate pressed her lips together. "Certainly not. I just hate to see him upset. Okay, maybe sometimes he worries me a little when he does the growly thing."

"He's a pussycat," Kellen said.

"Okay, so *you* move the pussycat."

Kellen took hold of Beast's two front feet

and pulled. Beast growled low in his throat but refused to move or open his eyes.

"This is ridiculous," Kellen said. "This is like moving a bag of wet cement."

"Maybe there's a bagel left downstairs. We could lure him off with food."

"I ate the last bagel," Kellen said. "And this is a challenge. This is man against beast. I can do this." He grabbed Beast and wrestled him around until they were both lying lengthways on the bed. "Okay," Kellen said. "Now I just have to get him to move to his own side."

Cate clapped a hand to her mouth to keep from laughing out loud.

"I saw that," Kellen said. "If you laugh at me you'll pay."

"Oh, yeah? What would the price be?"

Kellen had a front foot and a back foot and was inching Beast along. "I don't know, but I'll think of something horrible. Like, you'll have to eat my cooking or meet my sisters."

"I could handle that," Cate said.

"You think you're pretty tough right now, but you've never tasted my spaghetti sauce,"

Kellen said, giving one last grunt and finally moving Beast to the edge.

Kellen kicked his shoes off and sat on the bed. He patted the spot next to him. "Come here, princess. Now I get to wrestle with you."

"Are you going to drag me across the bed by my feet?"

"No. I'm going to whisper erotic suggestions in your ear, and then I'm going to demonstrate."

Cate sat next to him. "You've had a full day, cowboy. Rescued me, solved a crime, tackled the beast. You might be too worn out to demonstrate."

Kellen grinned and twirled one of Cate's curls around his finger. "I think I can manage to dredge up some energy."

Cate unlaced her sneakers. "What will happen to Kitty? Will the police find her? If they do, I doubt her husband will do much to help her out."

"If she's smart, Kitty and her henchmen are at Logan right now, loading everything they can beg, borrow, and steal onto a private plane to some unknown and exotic location."

"About those erotic suggestions . . ." Cate said.

"What about them?"

Cate ran her hand under Kellen's shirt, enjoying the feel of his warm skin, letting her fingertips memorize the muscle definition. "I'm ready to hear them," she said. "*All* of them. And I want details."

Cate opened her eyes to sun peeking through the curtains in Kellen's bedroom. Kellen was gone, but Beast was at the bottom of the bed, Cate's foot trapped under him. Both the foot and the dog were dead asleep. Cate eased her foot out from under the dog and massaged some blood back into it. A small price to pay for a loyal companion, she thought.

She looked at her watch and grimaced. Almost ten o'clock. Half the day was gone! She was going to have to start a vitamin regimen if she was going to keep up with Kellen. He wore her out . . . in a *very* good way.

She took a long, hot shower and realized she hadn't any clean clothes. She rummaged through Kellen's dresser and came up with a T-shirt. The rest of yesterday's clothes would have to make it through the morning until she could get back to the condo and change. She fluffed her hair dry, and she and Beast plodded downstairs to the kitchen in search of breakfast.

A cereal box sat out on the counter. Plus coffee in a cardboard take-out cup. Cate stuck the cup in the microwave to reheat and read the sticky note on the cereal box.

WALKED AND FED BEAST AND GOT YOU SOME CEREAL. MILK IS IN THE FRIDGE. MARTY TURNED HIMSELF IN THIS MORNING. I'M MEETING WITH THE PROSECUTOR. WILL BE BACK SOON.

Cate poured out some cereal and added milk. She retrieved her coffee and ate standing up in the kitchen. There were papers accumulating on the counter, Kellen's cereal bowl in the sink, Beast's bowl on the floor, keys and loose change on the counter. One of those keys was for Kellen's front door. He'd left it on the counter for Cate. The kitchen was starting to have a life.

"I love this cozy little brownstone," Cate said to Beast. "And I know this is dumb because it's been such a short amount of time, but I love Kellen too. He makes me feel happy and sexy and safe. I thought I did a pretty good job of keeping a clear head and looking brave through all of this, but the truth is I was scared. Truth is, I kept going because I love you and Kellen, and I knew I had to fight to keep you both. Unfortunately, I'm not sure how Kellen feels about me. I know he likes me. And I know he's a good guy, and he's working hard to be nice to me. I just don't know how deep his feelings go.

"And just between you and me, I'm not sure this is such a great time in my life to be falling in love. I still have dreams about finishing school and teaching. And then there's *you*. I'm a new dog mommy. I haven't totally got it down. How am I going to juggle Kellen, you, school, and work all at the same time? What do you think?" Cate asked Beast.

Beast stopped drinking water. He looked up at Cate, water ran from between his lips, and he burped.

"You're probably right," Cate said. "A walk might help clear things up. Not to mention I need clean clothes."

Cate snapped the leash onto Beast's collar, and they headed out the door into the midday heat. They took it slow, leisurely strolling the route to Cate's condo, pausing occasionally in the shade to watch couples walk past on their way to Sunday brunch and families returning from church.

Cate had mixed feelings when they reached her building. It was home, but it had never really been home. Not in the same way her parents' house had been home. Not in the same way Kellen's house could be home.

"We're an odd pair," Cate said to Beast. "Sort of in limbo, but at least we have each other now. And maybe we have Kellen."

The lobby was empty, and the elevator ride was quiet. Cate rang Marty's bell and held her breath. No answer. She rang again and punched the code into the lock. She stepped inside with Beast and called out to Marty. She didn't know a lot about the process when someone confessed to a crime. She supposed they went to jail, but maybe not right away.

"Anybody home?" Cate called a second time.

No answer.

Cate resisted the urge to snoop in Marty's bedroom and check his closet for telltale signs of a last-ditch flight to Buenos Aires. Instead, she led Beast straight to her little room, where she changed into clean clothes and packed a few more essentials into a bag, just in case Kellen wanted her to stay longer.

Cate locked up after herself and took the stairs to the third floor. She knocked on Julie's door. No answer. She knocked on Sharon's door. No answer.

"Nobody home," Cate said to Beast. "We'll have to visit some other time."

Chapter
NINETEEN

Kellen was working at his laptop when Cate and Beast came into the kitchen.

"I have a suite of offices," he said, "but I like working here, at the table. It's comfortable."

There were two sandwiches on the table and one in Beast's food bowl, complete with chips and a pickle.

"I see you cooked lunch," Cate said to Kellen, smiling at the Beast bowl.

Kellen grinned back. "I thought he deserved a special treat for being such a good guard dog."

"How'd it go today?"

"Great. Marty confessed to everything and turned in the pieces he had locked away. I think the prosecutor really felt for him. Plus, the prosecutor was a fan. He said Marty once sang 'Happy Birthday' to him Marilyn Monroe–style. And here's the best part. Turns out one of Kitty's charities is the Police Benevolent Association. And if that isn't enough, Kitty and Marty have been funding the Crime Stoppers program. Marty's Robin Hood defense hit close to home. Marty will probably only have to serve six months in jail, a year on probation and a hundred hours of community service. They specifically mentioned performing at seniors' homes and the annual Policemen's Ball."

"That's fantastic."

"I know. That means we can plan our wedding for the fall of next year."

"What?"

"Our wedding. Remember a couple nights ago when we got engaged and had some incredibly hot and passionate gorilla sex?"

Cate was speechless. Surely he was joking.

"I figure by next fall you will have graduated and be ready for your next challenge, namely me. But I don't think we should wait too long to get you a ring. After last night I'm a little worried about Pugg taking over as your hero."

Cate tilted her head back and laughed. "He does lead with his heart. But I think, in the end, Pugg's heart belongs to Julie."

"And how about your heart? I love you, Cate. I love the way you find something good in everyone. I love the way wherever you are feels like home. I even love your big, goofy dog." Kellen picked a large box up off the floor and placed it on the counter in front of Cate. It was wrapped in white paper with a green ribbon and a Williams-Sonoma sticker. "And possibly most of all I would love to try one of those fantastic cakes I've heard so much about."

Cate looked at Kellen, and slid the ribbon

off the box and then the paper. Inside were two cake tins, a hand mixer, a spatula, and some red oven mitts.

"I'm not sure what else you need," Kellen said. "But I thought this was a good start."

"It's a great start!" Cate said. "It's so sweet of you. It's the perfect gift. It's symbolic and sensitive, and it even has a whisk attachment. I've always wanted a mixer like this."

Kellen hadn't actually noticed the whisk attachment, but he was glad Cate liked it. For that matter, Kellen hadn't previously seen the symbolic importance of the gift. Although now that Cate pointed it out to him he was pretty damn impressed. Truth is, Kellen had just wanted a cake. He was hoping it would be chocolate with lots of those colorful sprinkles on top.

A tear slid down Cate's cheek.

"Is that a good tear or a sad tear?" Kellen asked.

"A good tear. It's one of those hormonal things."

Kellen had a bunch of sisters. He knew all about hormonal things, so he hugged Cate to him. "Will you marry me?"

"Yes. Probably. Yes."

Kellen snuggled her closer. "Am I rushing you?"

"A little, but it's okay. We'll have a long engagement. Give you lots of time to back out."

"I'm not going to back out."

"Me either," Cate said. "I'm almost positive."

EPILOGUE

Cate stomped the freshly fallen December snow from her boots and crossed the lobby to the mailboxes. It was starting to feel like the holidays. There were garlands on the streetlights and wreaths on door fronts and twinkle lights everywhere.

Cate stuck the key into the box for 4A and removed a stack of catalogs, a couple of bills and some personal mail addressed to Marty.

The catalogs would get tossed. She'd pay the bills from the account Marty had set up for her. The personal letters she would put in a growing pile on the kitchen counter. Marty had preferred this to forwarding them to him. He was scheduled for a February release. He'd be out for Valentine's Day, and Evian was already advertising his first performance.

Better than Kitty Bergman's future, Cate thought. Kitty was still embroiled in a messy trial and an even messier divorce.

Cate was alone tonight. No Beast. No Kellen. They were at Kellen's townhouse, eating their traditional once-a-month guy's-night-out dinner in front of the television. And Cate was having her traditional once-a-month dinner with "the girls."

Sharon was hosting. That meant a cosmo when Cate walked through the door, and later a slab of Sharon's fabulous lasagna.

Cate took the elevator to the third floor and rang Sharon's bell. The door opened and the cosmo was offered. Cate took the drink and held it high. "Let the monthly meeting of 'the girls' begin," she said to Sharon and Julie.

"To the girls," they said in unison, and each took a ladylike sip of their cosmo.

"It doesn't feel right that you're not in the building anymore," Julie said to Cate, "but at least we have our monthly."

"I stop by every day to get Marty's mail when I walk Beast," Cate said.

"Yeah, but it's not the same," Julie said.

"I agree," Sharon said. "And last week Julie was gone, and I was here all alone."

"You weren't alone," Julie said, gulping cosmo. "You were with the Mystery Man. You're always with the Mystery Man."

"It's true," Sharon said. "I have a boyfriend. A *serious* boyfriend."

"You always knew he was the one," Cate said.

Sharon nodded. "I had a feeling. And now that I know him I have a feeling it's going to last."

"How's it going with Mr. Yummy?" Julie asked Cate.

Cate settled herself in a club chair. "It's terrific. At first it all seemed so sudden, and I wanted to wait a while for the wedding, but now we're thinking about moving it up. We've been living together for almost four months, and I can't imagine life without him."

"I know just what you mean," Julie said. "I've gotten real used to havin' Patrick around. It's like havin' a big ol' bear in the house. And the best part is he can make pancakes. And last week we went home to my cousin Shirley's wedding and Patrick was a big hit. Shirley had her wedding in Uncle Ed's garage and they had a luau theme. You should see Patrick hula dance. I swear, you'd think a person'd need a waist for that, but turns out he don't. Patrick says he's so good at it on account of he studied that ritualistic gooney bird dance. I think Patrick just has natural dancin' talent. He's got a real good sense of rhythm, if you know what I mean."

"I'll drink to that," Sharon said, setting a bowl of nuts on the coffee table and taking another sip of cosmo.

"And after having said those nice things about Patrick I have two excitin' things to show you girls," Julie said. She stuck her left hand out and displayed a ring. It was a platinum band dotted with tiny diamonds.

Cate and Sharon gasped at the ring.

"It's not!" Sharon said.

"It is," Julie said. "We got married when we were in Birmingham. He was just so cute doin' that hula gooney bird dance that I lost my head. And that isn't all. I have somethin' else to show you." Julie pulled an envelope out of her pocket. "Look at this! It's my first ever check from my publisher. My book won't be published for a whole year yet, but I got a check for signing. It's not like it's millions or anything, but it's a start. And I can buy a couch and a bed now. Patrick'll like that. Poor thing's wearing the hair off his knees."

Cate raised her glass again. "To Julie!"

"To all of us," Julie said. "We're like the three princesses who found their Prince Charmin's and lived happily ever after."